TAMPERED

A RYLIE COOPER MYSTERY

STELLA BIXBY

FERRY TAIL PUBLISHING LLC

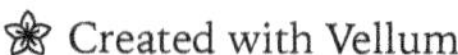 Created with Vellum

For my sweet Faith. I don't know if you'll ever read this, but if you do, I hope you know how much I love you.

(Hint: It's way more—but different, of course— than Jim loves Pam.)

What had I done to deserve this?

Every part of me wanted to cry. To hide in a prairie dog hole and never come out.

But hiding wasn't an option. I had to stay strong. They could sense fear.

If I could make a gruff old fisherman smile after writing him a ticket, this should be nothing.

It wasn't nothing.

It was ten tweenagers with chips on their shoulders and community service hours to complete. It was a spring break program the courts had determined would help them build character.

It was all Nikki's fault.

Just when I thought we were becoming friends, bam, she hits me with this. And I couldn't say no. I'd been in a room with the director—my big boss.

So I'd agreed. Stupidly.

I should have said no, even if that made me look like

less than a team player. I'd rather have the director mad at me than hang out with a bunch of baby criminals.

Ugh.

"Where's the bathroom, *Rusty?*" a twelve-year-old boy with spiked hair and a shoplifting habit asked.

"It's Rylie," I corrected for the umpteenth time. "And the bathroom—or rather—the port-o-potty is on the other side of the hill." I pointed behind us toward the nearest portable toilet. "We passed it on the way over."

"I'm gonna need running water," he said.

"Sorry." I shrugged. "Can't help ya."

"Wait, are you saying there's no running water here?" the princess of the group with her bleach-blonde hair and over-tanned skin asked. She probably thought she'd be spending her spring break in Florida.

Mmmm . . . Florida sounded nice right about now.

"That's exactly what I'm saying," I said, shooing away thoughts of warmer weather. "It's not ideal, but it does the trick."

Spike crossed his arms. "I'll hold it."

"Great," I said, ignoring their attitudes. "As was stated in your informational packet, we have an opportunity to get this trail in better condition before the summer." I had memorized the speech Nikki prepared for me.

"Yeah, opportunity," Princess murmured to the girl next to her. "More like free labor."

"Legal slavery," Spike added.

I sucked in a breath and acted like I hadn't heard them. It wasn't like I enjoyed trail maintenance, either, but Shadow Trail Reservoir was known for its pristine walking trail.

Shadow Trail was the smallest of the three reservoirs owned by Prairie City, Colorado. It was a great fishery and hiking trail, but bikes, swimming, and anything motorized —besides the ranger vehicles—were strictly forbidden.

That also meant the park was incredibly slow, especially compared to Alder Ridge Reservoir—the park where I'd done most of my shifts since I was hired as a park ranger almost a year ago.

"We'll start by picking up trash." I pulled big black trash bags from my supply box. "You should have gloves."

The tweenagers looked around—their attitudes building off each other's like fire with an accelerant.

"Yeah, I didn't bring gloves," Spike said.

"Me neither," Princess said.

The others went right along with them.

"Good thing I have extras," I said.

Spike deflated when I handed him the first pair.

"Now take a bag and start filling it. The trail is five miles all the way around. I figure we should be able to get all the trash picked up by the end of the day so we can move onto something else tomorrow."

They groaned but took trash bags and started picking up trash . . . slowly.

I unzipped my jacket and pulled my phone from the pocket of my light gray button-down uniform shirt. Only one message from Shayla, my roommate and best friend.

spaghetti for dinner tonight?

I punched out a quick response before the kids caught me using my phone. They'd think I was a total hypocrite if

I was on my phone when they couldn't be. Granted, I wasn't the one who had broken the law and ended up with community service hours.

"Were you texting your boyfriend?" Princess said from behind me.

I slipped my phone back into my pocket. "What I'm doing is none of your business."

"Is he cute?" Her tone was teasing—I couldn't tell if she was trying to bully me or make me her friend. Either way, she was stalling, and there was no way I would talk to *her* about my love life.

"Your bag looks pretty empty," I said. "Better pick up the pace."

I turned to the group. "Whoever has the heaviest bag by the end of the day will get a special surprise."

"A special surprise?" Spike said. "How old do you think we are?"

That trick always worked on my nephews, but they were much younger than these kids. "I'll make it worth your while," I corrected.

"Cash," Spike said. "Or we walk."

How was this backfiring on me? Nikki told me to offer incentives but to be firm. Just as I was about to tell the little extortionist that he could walk his sorry ass right back to juvie, Princess called out to us.

"Hey, come look at this," she said.

The group meandered over to where she stood.

"Those look like mountain lion tracks." Princess pointed to what could have been any sort of tracks as far as I was concerned.

But the other kids' eyes were wide with excitement. Maybe I could use this to my advantage.

"There *have* been reported sightings of mountain lions in the park recently," I said. It wasn't a total lie—a woman who lived in one of the houses bordering the reservoir *had* called a few times to say she thought she saw something big. She assumed it was a mountain lion, but we'd never gotten any actual confirmation.

"We should follow them and see if they lead to a mountain lion cave," one of the boys said.

"Mountain lions don't live in caves," a girl said. "They live in trees."

Everyone looked up into the bare aspen trees surrounding us.

"We can follow the tracks," I said. "But along the way, we need to collect trash. Deal?"

They all nodded in excitement. Heck, I'd be excited if I thought I might come across a mountain lion too.

"What do we do if we find it?" Princess asked.

"Fall on the ground and play dead," Spike said.

"No," I said. "Do not play dead." Not that we would find one, but I figured I'd better at least give them solid advice. "You would want to make yourself as big and loud as possible. Don't turn or run. Don't look into their eyes. Just back away slowly."

"Do you think we'll see one?" Princess asked.

I shrugged. I didn't want to tell them that there was no chance of seeing a mountain lion in a group this large, in the light of day, in the middle of a city where there hadn't been any confirmed sightings. If I told them the truth, they wouldn't have the motivation to pick up trash at the pace they'd increased to.

"Maybe," I said. "But let's stick together. That way, if we do, we'll have numbers on our side, and it'll likely run away."

They nodded and stayed close. It was easier to see them this way, and whatever kind of animal we were following had conveniently walked right next to the trail. My guess was the tracks were probably made by someone's dog, but if the idea of tracking a big ferocious cat made the activity more fun, then so be it.

A yawn escaped my lips as a park visitor jogged by flashing his pass. "Thanks, Jacob."

He waved and continued down the path and out of sight. Every day, he ran into the park from who knew where, twice around the trail, and then back out. He'd introduced himself briefly the first time he'd seen me, insisting I call him by his first name, but other than that, we hadn't spoken much.

Unlike the chatty fishermen at Alder Ridge Reservoir, the Shadow Trail visitors seemed to keep more to themselves. Where Alder Ridge was a place for recreation and big fish stories, Shadow Trail was a place to relax and recharge. And in the cool spring air, it was an excellent place for an invigorating morning run.

About halfway around the trail, as the sun hovered high in the sky, one of the girls a few yards ahead let out a blood-curdling scream yanking me from my thoughts.

I froze.

Had she spotted a mountain lion?

Princess and Spike got to her before me. All three of them stood staring at a place a few feet off the trail.

"What's wrong?" I yelled, hurrying to where she was standing.

The girl's face was pale, her eyes wide, as she pointed to the ground. She pulled her jacket tight around her.

"Is—what is that?" I asked, peering closer.

Four fingers poked up through dirt and dead leaves as if reaching out for something to grasp.

"It's a zombie," Spike said.

"It's not a zombie," I said. "Zombies aren't real."

One of the boys leaned down to pick it up, but I stopped him. "Don't touch it," I said. "It could be part of a crime scene."

Another crime—especially a death—was the last thing I needed. But I couldn't think of another explanation.

"I'll call the police," I said, pulling out my phone and dialing Luke—my ex-boyfriend and local police officer—rather than the actual police station.

"Hello?" Luke said on the first ring. He had been my high school sweetheart, and about a year ago, I thought he and I might reconnect. Instead, he and Nikki—the ranger who had gotten me into this tweenage hell—had started dating.

"Are you busy?"

"If this is about Garrett, then yes, I'm busy." Luke's voice was distracted.

"No," I blushed, thankful the kids couldn't hear what he'd said. "This is official business."

"What do you mean official?" he asked. "Not another dead body, right?"

"Well . . ."

"Seriously?" He grunted. "Where are you?"

"At Shadow Trail."

"I'll call dispatch and be over shortly. Don't touch anything."

"Thanks. See you soon," I said in my most chipper voice so the kids wouldn't get more freaked out than they already looked.

"Shouldn't we dig it up?" Princess asked. "What if she's still alive under there?"

"What makes you think it's a she?" I asked.

"Fingernail polish." Princess pointed.

The skin on the fingers looked cracked and caked with mud, but a hint of dull red nail polish could be seen on a couple of the fingers. Patches of snow still covered where the rest of the body would be buried. "I think whoever is down there has been there a while." It would take the forensics team hours to get through the frozen ground to recover the body.

One of the girls threw up.

"How about we back away from the crime—I mean—the area." I motioned for them to follow me to the other side of the trail. "You can put your trash bags down and sit on the edge of the lake. We'll get back to picking up trash shortly."

The kids meandered over to the shoreline. Well, all but one. "You sounded cozy with the policeman on the phone," Princess said.

"He's a friend," I said, instantly regretting my admission.

Her eyebrows rose toward her hairline. "Is he cute?"

"Yeah, sure. But he has a girlfriend. And no—" I held a hand up, stopping her from asking anything else "—it's not me."

She shrugged as if she didn't care anyway, and joined the other tweens.

"Ranger Seven, Ranger Five," I said into the mic on my shoulder.

"Five," Antonio's voice echoed through the speaker. I chided myself when my stomach did a little flip-flop.

"I have a possible code fifty-five over here at Shadow Trail. The police are on their way."

"Copy." His voice was almost annoyed. We hadn't interacted much in the past three months.

Not since he kissed me on Christmas Eve.

L uke wasn't the first to arrive at the reservoir. In fact, he wasn't even in the top ten.

Apparently, sending the kids to sit on the shoreline by themselves gave them permission to start texting their parents and friends.

I was blissfully unaware until I noticed two men approaching—one with a rather large camera slung over his shoulder.

"I'm sorry." I held up a hand to stop them. "This part of the trail is closed."

The better-dressed man held up a microphone, and the other leveled the camera directly at my face.

"Are you the ranger who found the dead body?"

I did not need this today. "I have no comment on what has or hasn't been found. Please wait in the parking lot until our public information officer gets here."

Just another person I'd need to call.

"Isn't it true you've found a record number of dead bodies over the past year?"

"Me?" I asked, defensive, even though it was true.

"We have word that there have been at least three, if not more, dead bodies in Prairie City parks over the last year."

"Again, you'll have to speak to our PIO." I put my hand up to the camera, forcing him to turn it off. "You can wait in the parking lot."

The man asking the questions gave a curt nod before turning and walking away.

He was replaced with a group of angry-looking adults.

"Can I help you?" I asked.

They all started talking at once.

When the tweens saw them, some rushed to hug their parents, and others just stood next to them.

"We're taking our children home," Princess's mother shouted even though she was only a couple of feet from me. "This is the last thing they need. Dead bodies. They'll have nightmares for months."

"Of course you can take your children home," I said. "After the police have had a chance to speak with them." If there could be anything good about finding a body, it was that I'd get out of babysitting these little hoodlums.

"Do you think the mountain lion killed her?" Spike asked.

All the parents' eyes widened.

"What mountain lion?" one of the fathers asked.

"There are no confirmed reports," I said.

"There have been reports of mountain lions, and you have our precious babies traipsing around picking up trash?" one of the mothers said.

"Like I said, the reports have not been confirmed," I said. "They were likely large housecats or dogs."

"But we saw the tracks," Spike said. I couldn't tell if he was excited about the prospect of there being a mountain lion or if he was intentionally trying to get me in trouble.

"Those tracks could have been from anything." I let out a nervous laugh. "Probably a dog or—"

"I will be contacting your supervisor," Spike's mother said.

Luke and his partner, Jerry, walked around them toward me. They were the odd pair—Luke tall and gorgeous, Jerry short and stalky.

"Ooh, he is cute," Princess said with a wink before her mother called for her to follow.

Luke blushed.

Jerry rolled his eyes. "Where is it?" he asked in his bullfrog voice.

"Right over here," I said. "We didn't touch it. At least, I don't think anyone did. I guess the kids could have touched it before I got here. One threw up close to it, but not directly over where the body would be."

"Where were you when they found it?" Luke asked.

"I was just behind them on the trail. They're hanging out so you can talk to them."

"Great, thanks."

"Unless you need me," I said. "I'll head up to the ranger office to keep an eye on the parking lot."

"Don't let anyone back here except the forensics team," Luke said, following me toward the group of parents and kids as Jerry inspected the fingers more closely with his gloved hands. "And when we're done with this, I need to talk to you about something."

"About what?" I asked, but Luke had already started talking to one of the mothers.

Jacob was coming around the corner for his second loop as I started to head back toward the office.

"Sorry, the trail's closed," I said with a half-smile.

He took his earbuds out. "What's going on? Is everything okay?"

"Everything is fine," I lied. "I'm sure the trail will be open again tomorrow."

He wiped his palms on his pants as he tried to see around me. "Was it one of the kids?"

"The kids are okay," I said, my tone more agitated than I wanted it to be. I took a breath.

He returned his gaze to me and smiled. "That's good." Though he wasn't especially good-looking, his smile could be featured on a toothpaste commercial. "I'll see you tomorrow, then."

He stuck the earbuds back in and resumed his jog back the way he came.

News trucks, police cars, and city vehicles packed the tiny gravel parking lot when I got back to the office. The PIO was giving an impromptu news conference, basically saying we had no information but would be distributing a statement when we did.

Thankfully the parents and their kids were gone. A twinge in my gut told me this might just get me fired—taking kids on a mountain lion hunt leading to a dead body—but I'd only been doing what they'd instructed.

"What'd yeh find this time, Blondie?" Seamus, one of

the other park rangers, asked in his deep Irish brogue when I unlocked the small two-room office.

"Fingers," I whispered so the news people couldn't hear. "Sticking out of the ground."

Seamus laughed as the forensics team approached.

I pointed them back to the scene. "It's about a half a mile or so down the path."

They nodded and walked toward where Jerry and Luke had stayed.

Seamus shook his head, his scruffy hair flopping around like a big shaggy dog's. "Only you."

"Technically, the community service kids found them." I walked behind the counter in the office and plopped down on a stool.

"Let me know if yeh need anything," he said, walking out the door. "See yeh for spaghetti tonight."

"If I'm not tied up here," I said.

Seamus and Shayla had been dating several months. He was a regular fixture in our apartment.

When the door was closed, I pulled the diamond ring from my pocket. It still didn't feel quite right on my finger, but that's where it belonged.

I made the excuse that it could get damaged in my line of work, but deep down, I knew guilt was the real reason I didn't wear it all the time.

I shoved it back inside my pocket for safe-keeping.

Within two hours, Luke, Jerry, and the forensics team came walking up the path carrying a single duffle bag. I was sitting on the front steps of the office, watching a group of geese waddle around.

Luke branched away from the group and headed straight for me.

"What's going on?" I asked. "I expected to be here late."

He glanced back at Jerry, who was getting mobbed by the cameras.

"Good news," Luke said. "It wasn't a body."

"What do you mean it wasn't a body? I saw the fingers."

"It was an arm. A prosthetic arm."

That would explain the weird cracking of the skin. "How did it get here?"

"Who knows? We'll have to check the serial number to see who it belongs to. We'll work from there."

"Were there any other clues? Any blood?"

"No blood." He laughed. "Which is a good thing."

"Of course, it is," I said.

"The arm did look battered, but that could be because it's been buried for a while."

I pulled out my ponytail and redid it. My hair was getting obnoxiously long. I was considering going short—real short—and maybe instead of blonde highlights going for a red.

"Don't look so sad," Luke said. "It's good it wasn't a body."

"I know," I said. "But that means the kids will be back. Let your girlfriend know how much I appreciate that one."

"She's not my girlfriend anymore," Luke said, not looking at me.

I stopped fiddling with my hair.

"Nikki and I broke up this morning," he continued.

He looked so sad. I wanted to hug him, but with all the people around, it didn't seem like the best idea. Instead, I reached out and rubbed his arm. "I'm sorry. What happened?"

"I'll fill you in later," Luke said. "I need to get back."

The last few weeks, he and Nikki had both confided in me about how they weren't happy with the other one. Their breakup seemed inevitable.

But if that was the case, why was Luke so upset about it?

3

O nce the reservoir was back to its usual quiet self, I typed out a message to Nikki.

I heard about you and Luke. I'm sorry. If you need to talk or a drink, let me know.

Her response came almost instantly.

K

I so badly wanted to call Luke and find out what happened, but I needed to get on with my shift and get the reservoir closed so I could make it to dinner.

Oh and the community service project didn't turn out like you'd hoped.

What do you mean, it didn't turn out the way I'd hoped?

I could hear the anger behind the words on my phone screen.

The kids found a prosthetic arm. I thought it might have been a body, but it wasn't. And I may have told them there could be mountain lions here.

She might kill me, but it was better she heard it all from me.

I'll get it figured out.

That was it?

I waited for more to come, but it didn't, and I didn't want to push.

On my drive around the reservoir toward the end of my shift, I came upon the place where we'd found the prosthetic.

The forensic team left the hole uncovered where they'd dug up the arm. It was only about a foot deep—a pile of dirt off to the side. They must have had some powerful heaters to be able to get the arm out so quickly from the frozen ground.

I pointed the beam of my flashlight into and around the hole. The forensics team rarely missed anything, but if they thought this was a harmless find, they may not have been as thorough as they should have been.

When I came up with nothing in the hole, I walked further around it—past the cluster of muddy footprints.

What I was looking for, I didn't know. But something in me felt like there was more to this case than met the eye. Maybe it was the fact that the job had been relatively boring since the beginning of the year.

Or maybe it was my gut.

Just as I was about to give up, something shiny caught the beam beneath a pile of dead tree branches about ten yards from the hole. I pushed them aside with my foot to uncover a single sleek red stiletto. It looked expensive. Probably more expensive than my entire wardrobe.

I scanned the area but didn't find another shoe.

I snapped a picture and sent it over to Luke with the message:

Think this might be related to the arm?

I could almost hear his sigh.

I'll be there shortly. Don't touch it.

The clock on my phone told me I needed to get back to the office and close the gates. I'd easily be able to find the spot again.

I jumped on the ATV and headed toward the park entrance to wait for Luke. Once he was in the park, I closed the heavy, eight-foot-tall gate behind him to make sure no one else came in.

It was a relief Jerry hadn't come too. Even though we got along, he still wasn't my favorite person in the world. He usually treated me like an annoying gnat that he had to put up with because I had connections to Luke.

"Wanna jump on with me so we can get this done

quickly?" I asked Luke when he stepped from his police cruiser.

"Sure." He took the extra helmet and jumped on behind me.

No matter how hard I tried to be cool, being this close to Luke made me a tiny bit giddy. I told myself it was the cold making me shiver. Thankfully, the noise from the ATV prevented the need for conversation.

"It's over here," I said when I turned off the ATV.

Luke pulled an evidence bag from his pocket. "You just happened to find it?"

I shrugged. "Okay, so maybe I'd been looking."

"Don't have much faith in us, do you?" His voice was playful.

"I guess not," I said with a laugh. "But it surprised me that everyone left after they realized it was a prosthetic. I mean, who loses their arm?"

Luke stopped in front of the shoe and pulled on some gloves. "Her name was Selena Marquez."

"As in the Selena Marquez who went missing a couple of years ago?" My heart started to race. "And no one thought it would be a good idea to come back out and see if they could find anything else?"

"I'm sure someone would have come back eventually." Something in his voice wasn't convincing.

He picked up the shoe and put it inside the bag.

"What are you not telling me?" I asked, my hands on my hips.

"Nothing," Luke said. "I'll take this shoe back to the office and try to find out if it's related."

He quickly put his helmet back on and was climbing on the back of the ATV.

I didn't move.

"What?" he asked.

I raised my eyebrows. "Tell me the truth."

He sighed and took off the helmet but stayed seated on the ATV.

"You didn't hear this from me, but this investigation is going nowhere," he said. "So you might as well drop it."

"What do you mean it's not going anywhere? We just found the first lead in a case that's been cold for years."

"It's above my pay grade," Luke said. "But that's why Jerry's not here. I was told to pick up the evidence and let the guys upstairs handle the rest."

"Like the administration?"

"It doesn't matter. I have my orders."

"Well, I'm not a cop, and I want to know what's going on." I pushed my shoulders back. "Maybe I'll just look into this one myself."

Luke didn't respond right away as if he were contemplating my threat.

I remembered the photos of Mrs. Marquez on the news. She was pretty even after cancer took her arm and her long brown hair. She'd been declared cancer-free only days before she'd gone missing.

Her husband, the owner of Marquez Manufacturing—one of the largest manufacturing companies in the state—had made public pleas for her safe return. Even though she was cancer-free, she still needed medication, he'd said. The tears in his eyes had seemed so genuine.

"Maybe it was the husband," I said.

"Rylie, stop," Luke said, his voice serious. "I am telling you, you need to stay out of this one. I don't even know that the chief knows all the complexities in this case. It's been sealed."

"It can't just be sealed." I threw my hands up in the air. "There's new evidence. No one searched Shadow Trail Reservoir when she went missing. Their focus was on her home. On the other side of the city." I paused, giving Luke an opportunity to confirm, but he didn't say anything. "It *was* the husband, wasn't it? And he's using his money to cover it up. That big fat jerk didn't deserve her in the first place."

Luke stood from the ATV and put his hands on my shoulders. "Okay, seriously. You have to stop. You cannot investigate this one. You will have no one backing you up."

"Except you, right?" I gave him my best puppy dog eyes.

He dropped his arms to his sides. "I can't help you. Not anymore."

"What do you mean?"

"That's what I wanted to talk to you about." His voice was shaky.

"How does you not helping me have anything to do with your breakup?" I asked. I'd assumed he wanted to tell me about some big argument they'd had that led to the falling out. I didn't realize it had anything to do with me.

"I'm leaving for a while," he said.

"Leaving? To go where?" My heart thudded in my chest. Over the past few months, Luke had become more than the high school sweetheart I'd failed miserably at trying to get back together with. He'd become my friend.

"I've been accepted to go to the Middle East."

Tears sprung to my eyes. "What do you mean you've been accepted?"

"I told you I signed up."

"And I thought it was a long shot."

"I did too. Until they called me."

"But can't you tell them no? You have a life here. You have a girlfriend and a job and . . ."

I wanted to say me, but my voice cracked.

"It's a commitment I made when I signed up. My job will still be here when I get back."

"What about Nikki?"

"She and I have been on shaky ground since December. You know that. It was only a matter of time before we ended things."

"So you're just going to leave? What if something happens to you? What if you die?"

He pulled me into a hug. I let the tears that had been held up in my eyes fall down his uniform shirt.

"I won't die. I'll be back. I promise," he said.

"You can't promise that. It's like promising someone you'll find their loved one's killer. You don't know."

Luke laughed. "I do know. My assignment is in a very low conflict area."

"How long?"

"Two years," Luke said.

My heart fell. In two years I'd be married. Maybe even have a baby on the way. We'd practically be strangers.

"When do you leave?"

"Next week."

"Do you get to come home for the holidays?"

"I don't know the specifics yet," he said. "But if I do, I'll make sure I see you. Okay?"

He looked like he wanted to kiss me. Part of me wanted to kiss him. But that was probably just residual feelings from our past relationship. They always said you don't ever get over your first love.

"But you have to promise you'll stay out of this case. That you'll try to stay safe while I'm gone. I've done a lot to protect you over the past year. Jerry won't do that."

I couldn't promise him I'd stay out of it. It wasn't that I wanted to put myself in danger, but if no one would look into Selena's disappearance because of some stupid politics, then I'd have to.

"Rylie?"

"I can't promise that," I said. "I'll be careful but—"

"Your idea of careful differs from mine by quite a bit."

"Says the man who volunteered to go to a war-torn country to what? Train some people to be cops?"

"I needed a change. And I'll be able to save a ton of money this way. By the time I'm back, I'll have enough to buy a house free and clear."

I didn't want to hear about how fantastic this opportunity was for him.

"I should go," I said. "Shayla's making spaghetti."

"I know. She invited me too."

Perfect. Now I'd get to spend the entire night acting like everything was okay when a man I cared for a great deal sat across from me, preparing to sacrifice two years of his life.

4

Thankfully, Luke had to take the shoe to the station before coming over. If we walked in together, Garrett would probably get all grumbly, and that was the last thing I needed after the day I'd had.

Ever since I'd broken Garrett's trust, he'd been a bit on the suspicious side. Not that I blamed him. In response to his proposal Christmas Eve, I told him I'd just kissed another man.

Luke had been my makeshift counselor since I'd royally messed up with Garrett. If it wasn't for his advice, Garrett and I wouldn't even be on speaking terms. Not that I could tell Garrett that.

When I opened the door, Fizzy and the smell of rich marinara sauce hit me like a ton of bricks. "Hey buddy." I scratched behind my pit bull Lab mix's ears. "Were you a good boy today?"

Shayla walked around the corner in light blue jeans

and an off-white wool sweater. Her curly blonde hair was tied back in a ponytail. "He was a saint, like always."

Shayla usually worked nights for Prairie City Police Department, but tonight was one of her nights off.

"Garrett and Seamus are in the dining room. We were starting to wonder when you'd get here."

"I got caught up at the reservoir. I'll tell you more about it later," I said, though I would probably leave out the part about Luke leaving. That wasn't my story to tell.

"I invited Luke and Nikki too," Shayla said. "But I haven't heard from either of them."

"Luke's coming," I said. "Nikki probably isn't."

Shayla's big eyes widened. "Uh-oh. Trouble in paradise?"

"Something like that." I pulled my coat and work boots off. "I'll change into something else and be right in."

Our apartment was a two-bed, three-bath in a beautiful part of Denver. Usually, the rent would be astronomical, but I'd become friends with the owner, and she'd cut us a deal.

My bedroom had light gray walls, a queen-sized bed that I never made, and an attached bathroom where I occasionally soaked in the massive bathtub.

I hung my bulletproof vest and button-down shirt inside my closet and pulled out one of my favorite Denver Broncos hoodies. A pair of jeans and a brush through the hair completed the look. If I hadn't been so hungry, I would have fixed my makeup too.

Just as I was walking out, I remembered the ring in the pocket of my work pants. Panic rose in my chest. What if it fell out when I took them off?

I reached into one pocket. Nothing. Then the other. My fingers landed on something hard and circular.

"Thank goodness," I said under my breath and pushed the ring onto my finger. It wouldn't feel so weird if I wore it more often. Soon, I'd never take it off.

"There she is." Garrett stood and pulled out a seat for me when I walked into the room. "I hear you had an eventful day."

"Just a prosthetic arm," I said, kissing him quickly.

"Did yeh get everything finished at the reservoir?" Seamus asked.

"Yeah," I said. "Have they said anything on the news?" I didn't want to give anything away about the investigation that wasn't already public knowledge.

"One of the stations said it was from a mountain lion attack," Shayla said, a smile spreading across her face.

"That's because the kids I was supervising found some tracks they thought were mountain lion tracks which led right to the arm," I said. "But I'm almost positive they were just dog tracks."

"We have had reports of a mountain lion over there," Seamus said. "Do yeh think they could be related?"

"Doubt it," I said.

"But if it was a mountain lion attack," Garrett said, "it wouldn't have eaten the prosthetic. Maybe that was all it left behind."

I glanced over to determine if he was being serious, but he burst out laughing. The rest of us joined suit.

"What's so funny?" Luke asked, walking into the dining room. He held a small bouquet of flowers and patted Fizzy on the head. "These are for you," he said to

Shayla. He was sucking up so she wouldn't be mad at him for leaving the country for two years. Sometimes men were so stupid.

"Thank you," she took the flowers to the kitchen to put them in a vase.

"Sounds like yeh had a busy day," Seamus said.

"Just more of the same," Luke said, brushing it off. "Dinner smells wonderful, Shay."

She walked out, holding the flowers in one hand and a casserole dish in the other.

"Let me help yeh with that." Seamus jumped up and took the casserole dish.

"Thanks," she said with a smile and a kiss on his cheek. He blushed. They were way too cute together. It made me want to gag.

Garrett squeezed my hand before letting go and dishing us both up a helping of spaghetti, salad, and green bean casserole.

"You went all out tonight," I said. "What's the occasion?"

"I just felt like cooking," she shrugged.

Luke glanced up at her as if he knew something more than she was saying. If anyone would, it was Luke since they both worked for the Prairie City Police Department.

Shayla was the epitome of a professional when it came to being a police officer. She hadn't once talked about a case, a suspect, or a victim. If something had happened on the job, she would never disclose it.

I didn't need to know the specifics to know something was wrong, though. Shayla always took her anxieties out in the kitchen. Not that I was complaining because she was amazingly talented with food, but it seemed she was making more and more casseroles these days.

"Well, it's delicious," Garrett said, wiping his mouth.

I took a swig of beer and did my best not to think about the conversation I'd had with Luke at the reservoir. He was leaving in a week, and here he was acting like nothing was wrong. The news would destroy Shayla. Who knew how many fancy dinners she'd cook up after finding out.

We finished dinner with basic small talk. Luke didn't bring up his news, and we didn't talk about the prosthetic case.

"I should go," Luke said after we'd indulged on ice cream sundaes. "Shayla, could you walk me out?"

"Sure thing," she said. Seamus didn't seem to mind her spending time with Luke one-on-one. Garrett definitely wouldn't have been so laid back.

Then again, Shayla hadn't kissed any other men since she and Seamus started dating.

"What's that all about?" Garrett asked when the two of them exited the apartment.

"Probably work stuff," I said.

"Has she talked to yeh at all about what's happenin' at work?" Seamus asked.

I shook my head. "No. She keeps everything pretty quiet."

"She won't tell me either," Seamus said. "I guess it's a good thing she can talk to Luke. He's a good lad."

She wouldn't have him to talk to for long. "Doesn't she have a training officer?"

"Her TO's not much of a talker from what I've gathered," Seamus said. "He wants to check the boxes and get her out of his hair."

"What about her mom?" Garrett asked. "She used to be a cop, right?"

"Her mom's not the warm and fuzzy type. To anyone. I don't think she'd be very open to listenin' to Shayla complain about the job." Seamus took a swig of beer. "Plus, Shayla is determined to prove herself to her mother."

I didn't envy Shayla's position. Sure, my mom could be overbearing, but at least she didn't expect me to be some sort of superhero.

"Hey." I turned to Garrett. "Are you staying over tonight?" He typically didn't stay over on weeknights, but I didn't want to be rude and not invite him.

"Nah, I have an early day." He glanced at the watch he'd worn since the day I met him. "I should get going. I'll thank Shayla on the way out."

He bent down and kissed me, making me both wish he was staying and blush because Seamus was sitting right there. "I'll see you tomorrow," he said before letting himself out.

I smiled and looked down at my hand. I could handle kisses like that every day of my life.

"I take it he's gotten over the whole cheatin' thing?" Seamus said when Garrett had gone.

"I didn't really cheat. I mean, I kissed someone else,

but it wasn't like I was dating someone behind his back or anything."

"That's still cheating, Blondie," Seamus said.

"Okay, fine. I cheated." Ugh. I hated that I was now part of the cheaters club. If anyone knew how it felt to be cheated on, I did. I was as bad as my ex and giraffe girl. "But yes, he's gotten over it. Or at least he's getting over it."

"I would hope so since he gave yeh that rock anyway."

"It was one stupid moment in my life, but it won't happen again. Heck, I've only seen Antonio a handful of times in group settings since Christmas Eve. It's not like we're even friends."

"It surprises me that Antonio kissed yeh, and that was that," Seamus said. He and Antonio had worked together for years. He knew Antonio better than most people.

"I think he realized it was a mistake." It didn't feel great to know that someone thought kissing me was a mistake, but it was for the better. "No harm, no foul."

"Mark my words, he'll be back for more," Seamus said in the most nonchalant voice I've ever heard from him.

"What do you mean he'll be back for—"

The door banged open, interrupting my statement. Shayla stormed into the room, mascara tears running down her bright red face.

Seamus stood and took her into his arms. "What happened, love?"

Shayla didn't say anything, she just sobbed. It had to be about Luke leaving for two years, but if it wasn't, I didn't want to let the cat out of the bag.

I rubbed her back. "What's wrong?" I asked.

Finally, she pulled back and looked at me. "Luke's leaving."

I nodded.

"Luke's leavin'?" Seamus asked.

Shayla burst back into tears and buried her face in his shoulder.

"Luke is going to the Middle East for two years to train people to be police officers," I said.

"And he leaves next week," Shayla said between sobs.

Seamus looked confused and angry. "But why?"

"So he can buy a stupid house," Shayla said, throwing her arms in the air. "Like he needs a house more than he needs to be here for his friends."

That confirmed my theory on Luke being her only source of release when it came to work issues.

"Rylie and I are here for yeh," Seamus said. "I know we're not cops, but we know how to listen too."

His voice was completely free of jealousy. It was a wonder he wasn't feeling a bit taken aback by his girl-friend being so upset over a guy she'd had a crush on for years.

"I know, but I can't talk to you guys. I wish I could, but confidentiality and all," Shayla said. "And my TO is awful."

"Do you want some more ice cream?" I asked. "Or maybe a drink?"

"I made a cake," Shayla said.

Not just any cake. It was a two-tiered chocolate-on-chocolate delight. It could have been in a bakery window.

Whatever was bothering her at work was way bigger than I had initially thought.

5

By the next morning, the news had picked up the information that the arm was from Selena Marquez. I sat in my comfiest yoga pants and sweatshirt eating a bowl of Lucky Charms as I watched the two news anchors discuss the break in the case.

"Though we've reached out to Jacob Marquez, owner of Marquez Manufacturing and Selena's husband at the time of her disappearance, we have not gotten an official statement from him," one of the anchors said.

My phone lit up with a text message.

Luke.

Please tell me you aren't the leak.

It was too early for a riddle. My brain hadn't even gotten its morning dose of sugar and caffeine yet.

What do you mean?

It's all over the news. The arm belonging to Selena Marquez.

Anger crept into my chest. Why would he think I'd have leaked the information?

I'm not the leak.

I typed the words into my phone with more force than was necessary, hit send, and flung it to the other side of the couch.

I didn't need his accusations. I was tired from listening to Shayla cry over *him* all night. Our apartment might have been nice, but the walls were paper thin.

I was looking forward to a quiet shift.

But the minute I pulled up to the gate, I knew that wouldn't be the case.

Police cars were parked inside the fence while vans from the three major news stations waited for the gates to open.

"What the hell is going on?" one of the early-morning fishermen said when he pulled through the gate I had just unlocked.

"I'm not sure," I said.

"Well, it damn well better not mess with my fishing."

Heaven forbid. I smiled and told him to have a good day.

"Rylie Cooper?" a police officer I'd never seen before approached me as I opened the trunk of Cherry Anne, my red Ford Mustang. He was tall and skinny and looked to be in his mid-fifties. His uptight saunter and straight face made it seem like he had a chip on his shoulder.

"That's me." I pulled out my duty belt and affixed it to the inner Velcro belt I was already wearing. "What's going on? Officer—"

"*Detective* Bryant," he corrected. "We have half of the trail blocked from visitors so we can process the crime scene you found yesterday."

Oh sure, *now* it was a crime scene.

"Okay," I said. "Do you need anything from me? I can show you where I found the shoe."

"No," he said in an overly assertive voice. "I need you to stay in the office or on the other side of the reservoir."

"But I—"

"No buts." He frowned. "I know you have something of a friendship with Luke Hannah."

"Luke and I go way back," I said. "I've helped on several cases recently."

He didn't seem to hear my words. "But your assistance will not be needed on this case or any cases in the future. It is in your best interest to stick to what you've been hired to do. If you'd like to become an officer, you can go through the academy and make your way up the ranks like the rest of us."

Ouch.

"Is that all?" I asked. "It looks like I have some park guests I need to attend to."

He stared at me for a moment as if trying to determine whether his words had landed. "If you choose to interfere with this case, you will not only be arrested for impeding an investigation, I have it on good authority that you will be fired from your position as a ranger."

His threat nearly made my jaw drop. "Am I excused?" I slammed the trunk lid and walked away without his permission.

"What was that all about?" Jacob said as I approached the office. "I'm usually good at reading body language. It looked like that guy really hates you."

"It was nothing. He doesn't even know me." I steadied my nerves, trying to be as professional as I could after what *Detective* Bryant had said to me. "The trail is closed again today. I'm sorry."

"No problem." He smiled. "I can take another trail. I'll see you tomorrow."

"Hopefully, this will all be cleared up by then." I unlocked the office and started opening procedures while replaying the conversation with Detective Bryant in my head.

How could he tell me I couldn't help? I was the one who found the arm and the shoe after they'd written the case off. It would have been completely written off if the news hadn't gotten wind of who the arm belonged to.

In some ways, it made me *want* to take credit for telling the news after all. Selena deserved justice. And the more people told me not to help, the more I wanted to.

"Um, hello?"

The voice startled me so badly I almost dropped the handful of passes I had been organizing.

"Can I help you?"

The man, likely in his forties, looked like a timid puppy. As if he might wet himself at the slightest raised voice. "I'm not sure. Maybe," he said. "It was stupid to come here. Especially with all that going on out there."

"If you're looking to hike around the trail," I said. "You might want to come back another day. The police have that half of the trail closed down. But I can redirect you to another walking trail." I pulled out a trail map of the city.

"It's because of Selena, right?" He didn't seem to care about the trails.

"I can't discuss that, I'm sorry." The last thing I needed was for Detective Bryant to hear me telling park guests about the investigation.

His eyes now brimmed with tears.

"Are you all right?" I handed him a tissue. He blew his nose before throwing it in the garbage can.

"She's my sister," he said.

"Selena was your sister?" I refolded the map.

"*Is* my sister. She's still alive, I know it. And *they* won't tell me anything." He motioned toward the window. "I've called a dozen times since I saw it on the news this morning, and they kept telling me they couldn't disclose any details."

"I'm sure they're just keeping it to themselves so they don't jeopardize the investigation." Even I didn't believe my own words.

"It's because of that bastard husband of hers," he said. "He's responsible for her disappearance, and he's paying them to keep me out of it. I'd finally made strides with my therapist. I was working through the grief. Through the disbelief that the police would so obviously take a bribe from that-that criminal." He clenched and unclenched his fists. "But you know something, don't you? You can tell me, right?"

My gut twisted. This man was obviously concerned for his sister. And was getting shut out because of someone with influence and power. Just like I'd been shut out this morning with Detective Bryant.

It wasn't fair to keep information from her brother. Someone who seemed to care about her.

"I don't mean to be rude, but how do I know you're really her brother?"

"I have proof." He pulled out a couple of wrinkled photographs of two kids that resembled younger versions of him and Selena—him being several years older than her. "And here's my ID. Obviously, my last name doesn't match, but . . ."

His name was Desmond Pratt. I didn't know Selena's maiden name.

"Do you have a photo of the two of you as adults?"

He looked down at his feet. "Selena didn't like to have her picture taken."

This seemed a bit too weird for me.

"If I tell you anything, my job could be on the line."

"So you do know something. I won't say anything. I swear. I just want to know what happened to Selena. She was the most important person in my life. And I wasn't the best big brother. When she disappeared, it was like my world fell apart."

He seemed desperate. "Look, all I know is that we found her arm and a shoe."

"A *red* shoe?" His eyes lit up. "The news didn't say anything about a shoe."

Shit.

I shouldn't have mentioned the shoe. "It was red, yes. Does that mean something to you?" I shouldn't have asked. It was way too close to trying to investigate. But I wasn't necessarily interfering with anything. The police could just as easily talk to Desmond.

"The night she went missing, she was on her way to a fundraiser gala. She was wearing a black gown and red shoes."

"How do you know this?" Something about this guy was freaking me out.

"It was part of the police description. They talked about it on the news every night. Black gown, red shoes."

"If she was on her way to a gala, how did her arm and shoe end up here?" None of this made any sense.

"Your guess is as good as mine." He didn't look at me when he said this.

I glanced out the window just in time to see Detective Bryant approaching the office.

"Shit," I said. "If he asks, you were asking about fishing. That's it."

Desmond's eyes narrowed. "What's in it for me?" His timid voice was sharp now.

Was he serious? "What do you mean, what's in it for you?"

"I think you'll owe me a favor."

Detective Bryant was almost at the door now.

"Fine," I agreed. "I'll owe you one."

Desmond smiled as if I just offered him my firstborn. "I won't say anything."

The door opened to an angry-looking detective.

"Desmond Pratt," he said. "What in the world might you be doing here?"

"I wanted information about Selena's case," he said, his timid voice returning. "I've tried to call the station a dozen times this morning, but they wouldn't tell me anything."

"So you thought you'd be able to get information out of a park ranger?" Detective Bryant raised one eyebrow. "How did that go for you?"

I held my breath. If Desmond didn't pull through on this, I'd be screwed.

"She won't tell me anything either," Desmond said.

I glanced at Detective Bryant to see if he'd bought the lie.

"So I'll ask you," Desmond continued. "What is going on with my sister's investigation?"

"You know we can't disclose details," Detective Bryant said.

"Does that mean you've reopened the investigation?" Desmond asked.

"That means we're processing what we found."

"And what did you find?"

"All I can tell you is you're wasting your time here. This park ranger won't be able to tell you anything. She's not part of the investigation. And I won't tell you anything. You'll find out the same way everyone else will."

"Everyone except her ex," Desmond said, pointing outside to a limo that had just pulled through the gates.

"As you've been told before, Mr. Marquez will get no more information than you."

"He's the one who did this," Desmond said. "You and I both know it."

"If I knew that, the police department would have charged him with a crime. We don't know what happened to Selena. She could have disappeared of her own accord for all we know."

"Oh sure, she yanked her arm off, left a shoe behind, and ran away."

Dammit. He wasn't supposed to mention the shoe. That wasn't public knowledge.

"What shoe?" Detective Bryant asked Desmond, but his gaze was on me.

"I heard some of the officers talking about a shoe outside," Desmond said, his timid demeanor slipped back in place.

"Uh-huh, sure you did," he said. "I think it's time you go, Mr. Pratt."

Desmond looked like he might protest but instead turned toward the door stopping just before walking out. "I'm not done looking into this. If you won't tell me what's going on, I'll figure it out myself."

When Desmond was gone, Detective Bryant turned his entire focus on me. "I can't discuss this now because I have to go take care of Mr. Marquez, but if I find out you gave that nut job any information, you'll be inside a jail cell before the sun goes down."

My palms were sweaty. I wasn't typically intimidated by men, but Detective Bryant wasn't messing around. He was out for blood. My blood.

He stomped out of the office only to come between Desmond and a man who looked eerily familiar, and not because I'd seen him on TV. The Jacob Marquez I'd seen making pleas for his wife's return had been overweight by at least 100 pounds.

This man was in peak physical condition. He wore a suit and tie and was recognizable as the same man I'd seen only hours before, and every shift I'd had at Shadow Trail.

Jacob Marquez was the jogger who insisted I just call him Jacob.

"Whoa whoa, back up," Detective Bryant said, putting himself between the two men. "If I recall, there's a protection order between the two of you."

It looked like they might start a wrestling match right there in the gravel parking lot. Between the two of them, Jacob would definitely win. Especially with the brute of a security guard standing behind him.

The woman to Jacob's left—presumably his new wife—clutched his hand holding him back. She looked like a younger version of Selena—long brown hair and big blue eyes—only with a belly indicating she was close to giving birth.

The news crews swarmed the scene as if they were kids on a playground waiting for a fight.

"He can't be within one hundred yards of me," Desmond shouted.

Jacob's security guard wrapped his dinner-plate-sized hand around Jacob's arm to keep him back.

"Yes, because I will obviously murder you just like I murdered your sister, right?" Jacob yelled. His wife let out a small laugh, and Jacob turned and glared at her.

"Mr. Marquez," Detective Bryant said, rubbing sweat

from his brow. "It would be in your best interest to take Mrs. Marquez back to your limo and leave." He looked toward the news crews. "And all of you can turn off the cameras now. There's nothing to see."

No one turned off their cameras.

Desmond didn't move.

Jacob and his wife didn't leave.

"We want an update on the investigation," Jacob said.

"Like I just told Mr. Pratt, we cannot disclose any information on an open investigation."

"Ah, so the investigation has been reopened?" Jacob said, his voice icy.

"With new evidence, we had no choice." Detective Bryant looked like I felt earlier when *he* was threatening *me*. Jacob had always seemed so nice when he was jogging around the reservoir, but now he looked capable of murder.

"I'd like to make a statement to the press." Jacob turned away from Desmond and Detective Bryant.

The cameramen reacted instantly, pointing their lenses at him.

Jacob wrapped an arm around his pregnant wife's shoulders and pulled her close to him before training his face to look as sad and hopeless as possible. "I would like to thank the Prairie City Police Department for their determination and perseverance in the investigation into my wife's disappearance."

At the mention of his wife, his current wife shuffled her feet, but he held her tight to his side.

"I would like to ask again if anyone out there knows anything about Selena's disappearance, please call PCPD and let them know. Elodie—" he looked to the pregnant woman beside him "—has helped me work through so much grief, and as you can see, we are expecting our first child—a little boy." He turned his attention back to the camera as his wife looked up at him in shock. "But that does not detract from the fact that I loved—that I love—Selena. She was an incredible person, and someone I admired greatly. I know there is little chance that she's alive somewhere, but either way, I'd like to know." He looked behind him at Desmond. "We'd all like to know." He moved aside so the cameras could see Desmond. "This is Selena's brother, Desmond Pratt."

Desmond took a shaky step forward while Detective Bryant stood off to the side with an exasperated look on his face.

"Though Desmond and I haven't always seen eye to eye, we both want the same thing. Justice for Selena."

Desmond nodded.

"I will once again offer anyone with credible information a sizeable cash reward. Thank you."

He turned and shook Desmond's limp hand with a grim smirk while keeping his arm tight around Elodie, dragging her along with his every movement.

The cameramen got the last little bit of theatrics before they dropped their cameras to their sides. Each of them thanked Jacob for the information, looking star-struck as they spoke with him.

"What was that all about?" I asked, coming up next to Detective Bryant, who still looked annoyed with the situation.

He turned toward me. "That was an act. One that will

make my job even harder. And I don't need anything else making my job harder." He glared at me. "Including you. Don't forget what I said." He marched over to Desmond, Jacob, and Elodie and managed to usher them to their cars.

So much for trying to make nice.

The rest of my shift was rather boring. The police still had the trail closed and had set up tents around the area where the prosthetic had been found. It was apparent they didn't want anyone to know anything.

About ten minutes before I could lock the gates, a new wave of police cars came in to replace the old ones. Amongst them were Shayla and her TO.

"Hey," Shayla said when I walked up next to her. "How was today?"

"Couldn't tell you," I said. "I've been warned that if I have any involvement in this case, they'll put me in jail, and I'll lose my job."

Shayla looked at me wide-eyed. "What? Why would they say that?"

I shrugged. "Seems like not everyone appreciates my help. And now that Luke is leaving, they don't care about hurting my feelings."

"I'm sorry," Shayla said. "I wish there was something I could do."

"I wouldn't ask anything of you. You need to focus on getting through your rookie period. I would never jeopardize your job."

"Would you jeopardize your own?" she asked.

I shrugged. "If I did, would you take care of Fizzy for me?"

Shayla let out a nervous laugh.

"I'm kidding. Mostly," I said. "You should go, though. You don't want Detective Bryant to see you talking to me. He's the head honcho out here."

"Bryant is brutal. I'll see you in the morning."

I loaded the back of my car, locked the gate, and left without anyone giving a damn.

Garrett was waiting for me in the parking lot of our apartment complex when I got home. "Hey babe." He kissed me on the cheek.

"Hey," I said, leading him upstairs and into the apartment. "I need to shower, and then we can hang out, okay?"

"Sounds good. I brought Chinese food." He held up two bags of food. "I'll get it all dished up."

I wanted to tell him I'd much prefer to eat it directly from the box, but he was so used to having things done properly that I decided to keep my mouth closed and just do the dishes later.

The warm water and fragrant shampoo washed away all the frustration of the day. If I had to deal with another day of Detective Bryant sneering at me, I'd need more than a shower to regain my calm.

"I saw the newscast of Jacob Marquez today," Garrett said when I walked out and curled up on the couch next to him. I loved how I fit so neatly under his arm. I'd never been the shortest girl, but with him being so tall, I felt almost dainty.

He'd turned on one of our favorite sitcoms and had beautifully plated takeout Chinese food and beer on the coffee table. "Do you think he killed Selena?" Garrett asked.

"It doesn't matter what I think," I said. "I've been told to stay out of it. Or else."

"Or else what?" Garrett rubbed my back as I took a bite of the delicious food.

"I'll lose my job, go to jail—you know—things I don't want to happen."

"Sounds serious." His voice gave away his worry more than his words.

"It's stupid. I feel like they're punishing me for something I didn't do. I've *helped* in the last few investigations. I've *solved* the last few investigations. Sure, Luke gave me access to information I probably shouldn't have had, but it's not like I used that information recklessly." I thought back to today and the conversation I'd had with Desmond. That wasn't the most responsible use of information, but surely it wouldn't damage the case.

"I guess it's a good thing you won't be working this

case. Then I won't have to worry about you," Garrett said. Even though I knew he thought he was being sweet, it irritated me he didn't seem to be on my side. That he'd rather have me give up.

"I don't know that I won't be working the case," I said, unable to let it go.

"Why would you risk it?"

"Because a woman went missing and no one seems to be doing anything about it."

"On TV it looked like the police were doing lots about it. They had tents up around the site and everything. You don't have to be everyone's hero."

He had called me everyone's hero the night we ended up officially engaged. But at that time, he'd said it was a sweet quality as long as it didn't get me killed.

"Let's just watch the show." I hit the play button on the remote. I could feel his gaze on me, but I was done talking. I didn't need him telling me to stay out of it too.

The first time my phone lit up with a message from Luke, Garrett pretended not to notice. The second time he huffed. Then when it lit up with a message from a number I didn't recognize, he turned to face me.

"Are you going to check your messages?"

"I'm irritated with Luke, and I don't know the other number," I said. "I'm trying to enjoy my time with you."

"What if it's something important?"

I sighed and picked up the phone. I read Luke's messages first.

Sorry about this morning.

I hear you met Detective Bryant.

I didn't want to talk to him, so I backed out of his messages and opened the other one.

Rylie, it's Desmond. We need to talk.

"Who's Desmond?" Garrett asked, not even trying to keep the jealousy from his voice.

"Selena's brother."

"Selena? As in the woman who went missing?"

"Yes." How had Desmond gotten my cell number?

"Why is her brother texting you?"

I sucked in a breath. I had to have patience with Garrett. It wasn't his fault he didn't trust me. "He couldn't get any answers from the police today, so he came into the ranger office to see what I knew."

"And did you give him anything?"

"Unintentionally. But I don't think it'll do any harm," I added quickly.

"Do you think you can trust him?"

"I don't even know him," I said. "But I think he's in the same position I am. He wants to know what happened, but everyone is shutting him out."

"Don't you think if they knew what happened, they'd tell the public?"

"Jacob Marquez is a very powerful man. He has connections."

"Do you really think his connections could help him get away with murder?"

"I don't know." I clicked my phone off and put it back on the table where it stayed the rest of the time Garrett was there.

Thankfully, no more messages came in.

I responded to Luke's message the next morning while I watched the early news.

Detective Bryant is an ass.

Luke was probably asleep when the message went through, which was fine by me. It meant he wouldn't respond.

The news was replaying the on-the-spot news conference Jacob Marquez had created at the reservoir the day before.

I'd read Desmond's text more times than I could count. If I texted him back, it would be in writing that I was helping him and interfering with the investigation. If I called, they could subpoena my call history, but I didn't feel like they'd go that far just to catch me trying to help. I mean, what judge would grant that search warrant?

I would have to call him after the sun rose.

When I got to the reservoir to open it back up, Shayla

was just packing up for the night. It looked like they were finishing whatever search they'd done.

"Everything is cleaned up?" I asked her.

"Yep. The trail is clear for guests."

"Did they find anything else?" I asked, my voice hushed so only she could hear.

"You know I can't tell you that."

"Yeah. Sorry, I asked," I said. "I just really want to know what happened to Selena."

"We all do. There's not one officer or detective that doesn't want to solve this case." The clipped nature of her voice stung.

"I know, Shay. I'm sorry."

"It's fine. I just need to get some sleep." She looked behind me, and her posture straightened, her eyes opening a fraction wider.

"Everything tied up?" Detective Bryant asked from behind me.

"I believe so," Shayla said.

"Good." He nodded once.

"Do you not sleep?" I asked him.

"Of course I sleep," he said but didn't justify his answer. "The trail is clear. We should be out of the park within the hour."

"Thanks," I said.

He stared at me for a moment longer than necessary and walked away.

"Ugh," I said. "I hate that guy."

"He's just doing his job," Shayla said. "I gotta go. See you later."

She slid into the passenger side of the police cruiser without another look.

And if that wasn't frustrating enough, my phone buzzed with a message from Luke.

He's good at what he does.

What the hell? Were all the people in my life against me? Was this some sort of put-Rylie-in-her-place intervention?

I shoved my phone back in my pocket just in time to see Jacob come running into the park. He pulled out his park pass and flashed it at me. "Is the trail open today?"

His demeanor was not that of a man whose wife's prosthetic arm had just been found after she'd been missing several years.

"They just reopened it."

He smiled, returned his pass to his pocket, and began jogging again. I wanted to ask him a million questions, but Detective Bryant was watching, his gaze accusatory.

Before he could give me any flack for talking to Jacob— doing my job—I turned and walked into the office to begin my opening procedures.

When the police were gone, the only two vehicles left in the parking lot were an old rusty truck belonging to one of the regular fishermen and a shiny black Escalade. The sun was starting to warm the air when I began my first patrol of the day on the ATV.

"STOP!" a voice called out behind me as I was about to head down the trail.

I turned to find Jacob's linebacker-sized security guard coming at me like a freight train.

I hopped off the ATV, putting it between him and me, and reached for my pepper spray.

He stopped in his tracks. "Don't shoot. I'm deathly allergic to that stuff." His deep voice didn't sound scared, but the look on his face was.

I dropped my defenses only slightly. This man could have easily taken me out with a single flick of his wrist. "What did you need?"

"My boss, Jacob Marquez, is out there on his jog."

I nodded.

"He has an appointment in an hour. He's usually back by now."

Alarms sounded in my head. Was he out there messing with the crime scene?

"Did you try calling him on his phone?" I asked.

"No answer."

"I'm heading out to patrol. I'll keep an eye out for him."

The man, dressed in head to toe black, dipped his chin only slightly, his deep brown eyes flickering to my hand resting on the pepper spray at my hip.

"He didn't kill her," the man blurted out.

"I never said he did," I replied. "What was your name?"

"Cedric. I'm Mr. Marquez's head of security."

"I'm Rylie," I said, shaking his hand.

"Everyone thinks he killed her, but he didn't."

"How do you know for certain?" I was bordering very closely on investigating, but I couldn't pass up the opportunity to hear what Cedric had to say.

"He may be a lot of things, but he's not a murderer."

"It's nice that you believe the best in him. He's lucky to have a friend like you."

"He's not my friend," Cedric said. "I despise him."

Was he openly admitting he hated his employer?

"Don't worry. He knows I hate him."

"I would think he'd want the head of his security to like him. Or at least respect him."

"I do respect him. But liking him is not necessary. I can't let anything happen to him. If I do, my neck is on the line."

My suspicions turned. "Do you know what happened to Selena?"

He flinched slightly at her name. "No."

"Do you think she's dead?" I asked.

"She has to be. Why else would they have found her arm?"

"If you think she's dead, who do you think killed her?" I had blown up the line I'd been walking. I was now wholly into investigation territory.

His gaze trailed off to the reservoir behind me. "I'd put my money on the brother."

"Desmond? You think Desmond killed her?"

"She hated him," Cedric said. "He tried to see her hundreds of times. Every time she declined."

"And you think that made him kill her?"

"He's nuts. Doesn't seem like it, but he is." Cedric

shrugged. "Anyway, if you see Mr. Marquez, can you tell him he needs to get back here?"

And just like that, the conversation was over.

"I will," I said.

He turned and walked back to his SUV.

As I made my way around the reservoir, I considered what he'd said about Desmond. Something felt off. Like he had intentionally thrown Desmond under the bus to take some of the suspicion off Jacob.

But if he hated Jacob, why would he care if Jacob was convicted of murder.

Then his words came back to me. His neck was on the line if anything happened to Jacob. And I would venture to guess anything included going to jail.

I turned a corner toward where we'd found Selena's arm, fully expecting Jacob to be there. He wasn't.

I slowed for a minute to examine the scene. Behind me, the reservoir glistened in the sunlight. Was Selena's body—minus an arm—somewhere beneath the blue mirrored surface?

As I started back around the trail, I caught a glimpse of something—or someone—hiding behind a group of trees just beyond the arm.

"Hey," I yelled out. "Who's there?"

The person didn't move.

I pulled the pepper spray from my belt and held it down by my side. "Come out before I call in backup."

"Okay," a voice said. "I'm coming out."

From behind the trees, Jacob Marquez appeared, his face red and splotchy, his hands covered in mud.

8

"Mr. Marquez?" I said from the safety of my ATV. "What are you doing out here?"

"It's not how it looks," he said, wiping his hands on his black running tights.

"It looks like you're tampering with a potential crime scene." I didn't get any closer. He could easily have a weapon in his loosely fitted jacket.

"I dropped my phone. I'm nothing without my phone. My entire life is on that phone."

He was easily fifty feet off the trail. "And you just happened to drop it in the exact location where your missing wife's arm was found?"

He took a step toward me. "Do you have a phone on you? Maybe if you call it, we'll be able to hear it vibrate. I know it's close. My Bluetooth headphones are still connected."

"Cedric said you need to get back to the car. You have a meeting or something."

"See? If I had my phone, I'd have known that."

"How long have you been looking for your phone?" He'd been here since the gates opened at sunrise. Now the sun was climbing in the sky.

"How am I supposed to know? It's my clock too." His eyes were pleading now. "Please just call it."

"Fine, what's the number?" I replaced the pepper spray and pulled out my phone.

I punched the number into my phone, then we both listened.

One ring.

Nothing.

Two rings.

Nothing.

Three rings.

"Here!" he brushed away a couple of leaves and picked up his phone. "Oh, thank goodness. I don't know how to thank you."

I hung up before it went to voicemail. "You can tell me what you were really doing out there."

His eyes narrowed. "I was looking for my phone. It must have slipped out of my pocket as I was running by."

"You were running back there? Fifty feet off the trail?"

He ignored my questions. "Looks like Cedric tried to call a few times."

"Mr. Marquez?"

The air was still. The only sound was of birds chirping.

"I was curious," he finally said. "This is the first shred of evidence we've found related to Selena in years. I just wanted to check out the area myself."

"Did you find anything else?"

"No." Either he was a good actor, or he really felt defeated. "I don't know what I'd hoped to find, but—"

His phone vibrated in his hand, and he raised it to his ear. "Yes, yes. I know, Cedric. I'll be there shortly."

He deposited the phone back into his pocket.

"Sounds like the two of you have a rocky relationship."

"Did he tell you that?" Anger flashed over his features. "What else did he say?"

"Nothing." I held my hands up, motioning for him to stay back. "It was just the way you talked to him on the phone."

"He's my *employee*. I can speak to him however I wish. Especially when he forgets that I pay his salary."

"I'll let you get back," I said, not wanting to be around this man any longer than I had to.

Jacob closed his eyes as if he was counting to ten. "You won't tell the police I was out here, will you?"

I considered this. "Why wouldn't I?"

Anger flashed on his face again, but he took a breath and regained his composure. "I can make it worth your while. How much?"

He was going to pay me? To keep quiet? "I can't take your money."

"Sure you can."

"I won't cover for you. I'm not like everyone else." It felt both brave and dumb to stand up for what I believed. My chest constricted, and my heart raced.

"What do you mean, you're not like everyone else?" He smirked. "Everyone has a price. Name it. Ten thousand? One hundred thousand?"

He was willing to pay me $100,000 to keep my mouth shut? "The more you talk, the more guilty you sound."

"Look, I need to keep my name clean. I was already drug through the mud when Selena went missing. My company nearly folded. If I have to pay someone a hundred grand to save myself millions in lost revenue, I'd happily do so." He glanced at his phone. "I really have to go. My checkbook is in the car. You can just wait for me there. I'll run back."

He took off as I stood stunned. He couldn't possibly be offering me $100,000 just to keep my mouth shut, could he?

Jacob beat me back to the parking lot and didn't look pleased that I'd kept him waiting.

"I'll be quick," I said, shutting the ATV off so he could hear me. "I won't take your money." It pained me to turn it down, but it was the right thing to do. "But I won't say anything. Not yet, anyway."

"I feel like there's a catch," he said.

"No catch. But if a time comes that I need information, I'll call you. I do have your number, after all."

"Deal." He smiled then pushed the check into my hand. "But keep this anyway. Just in case you change your mind."

Cedric nearly closed Jacob in the door when he slammed it shut.

"You better be careful with that one," I said to Cedric.

"He knows better than to mess with me," Cedric said. "There's a reason he keeps me as head of his security."

As they drove away, I shoved the check deep into my pocket, parked the ATV outside the office, and smoothed down my hair from the helmet.

This day could not get any weirder.

9

Okay, maybe it could get weirder.

"Did you get my text last night?" Desmond barged into the office the minute I'd taken a bite of the leftover spaghetti I'd brought for lunch. He looked harried, his eyes shifty and almost scared.

I nodded my head yes.

"Why didn't you respond?"

I swallowed and wiped my mouth before speaking. "First of all, my fiancé was not thrilled about some random guy texting me. And second, I was not going to put in writing that I would help you."

"I didn't ask you to help me in the text. I just said we needed to talk."

"What we need to talk about is how you got my cell phone number."

"That's the last thing we need to talk about," he said. "Did you see the bruises on Elodie's wrists yesterday?"

She had been wearing a maternity dress with a big jacket and leggings. "I didn't see any bruises."

"There were bruises," he said. "I was standing right behind her. And did you see how he yanked her around? He always used to do that with Selena too."

"You don't have to convince me that the most likely suspect in this investigation is the husband," I said, thinking back to this morning.

"Don't you think we should warn Elodie?" Desmond asked.

"Warn her about what? I'm sure he won't kill twice." If he'd even killed the first time. "Plus, she's carrying his son. I doubt he would do anything to her, especially while she's pregnant."

"But what about afterward?"

I thought about it for a minute. "I don't know." I took another bite of my spaghetti. "Maybe he's changed."

"A leopard can't change their spots."

I shrugged. "Maybe not."

"I know you want to help me." His face twisted into what I assumed was his best pleading expression. "I need to know what happened to my sister."

"From what I hear, the two of you weren't as close as you pretended to be."

For the first time since he'd barged in, he seemed taken aback. "Who have you been talking to?"

"Doesn't matter," I said. "But if you weren't close, it makes me wonder why you care so much about this investigation."

"I'm not a suspect, if that's what you're implying."

"I'm not implying anything." I took another bite. I wouldn't let this guy get the upper hand in this conversation.

"The police cleared me. I had a verifiable alibi."

"Why would the police have looked into you in the first place?"

"I'm her brother. And yes, we were estranged. Our childhood wasn't great. Our dad was abusive, and I—" he stopped.

"You what?"

He looked like he might cry. "I left her there. I went to college and left her with that monster. I never thought he'd hurt her. She was his little girl. I was his annoying nothing of a son. But I guess without me to beat on, he needed someone else."

My stomach twisted. Selena had been through a lot.

"When Jacob showed up, she thought he was her hero taking her away from that place. And she never wanted to speak to me again."

"She blamed you."

"Of course she did. And she had every right to." He dabbed at the corner of his eyes. "And then she married a man just like our father. I thought it was my second chance to help her. Protect her. But she turned me away every time I tried."

"How do you know Jacob abused her?" I asked. His temper was evident that morning, but just because he had a temper, didn't mean he was abusive.

"I know the signs. I saw them with our mother before she died." He steadied his voice. "Jacob is the reason Selena is missing. I'm sure of it."

I wanted to ask how his mother died but didn't want to make things worse.

"Please help me. I know you want to."

I finished chewing and swallowed. "You're right. I do want to help. But I also want to keep my job and my friends and not end up behind bars."

"They can't put you behind bars for asking some questions," Desmond said.

Shayla's words echoed in my mind. "The police seem to have it under control." Betraying Shayla would be way worse than betraying Luke. Heck Luke would be gone in a matter of days. I *lived* with Shayla.

"The police have nothing under control. They're in Jacob's pocket. He throws money around like candy at a Fourth of July parade."

I knew this was true first-hand.

"The minute they stopped investigating the officers had new uniforms. That had to have cost a small fortune. And I know it didn't come from taxpayer money."

"What exactly do you want me to do?"

"I know you've helped with cases in the past. You seem to have the tenacity to get things done. I want to know you're on my side. Helping find Selena. We can share information and solve this case together."

"Information? What information?"

"You have contacts in the police department. You can get information I can't. And visa versa. Remember, you owe me one."

"After you practically told Detective Bryant that I told you about the shoe? I don't think I owe you anything."

He threw his arms in the air. "Fine, you don't owe me one. I'll keep your secrets. Just please, help me."

"What information can you provide me?" I asked.

"I don't have much yet."

I shook my head. This guy was impossible.

"But I'm talking to someone tonight. He says he has information about what happened."

"Who is this guy?"

"He's a private investigator. I hired him to look into Jacob and Elodie."

"And you think he found out who killed Selena?"

Desmond thought a moment. "I don't think Selena's dead."

Wishful thinking. No one wanted to believe their missing loved one to be dead.

"But I think he figured something out about her disappearance," Desmond continued. "I'll talk to him this afternoon. Maybe we can meet back here tonight, and I can tell you about it."

"Why here?" I asked.

But before he could respond, Luke walked in the door.

"Hello, Desmond." Luke peered down his nose at the man who looked like he might poop himself.

"Officer," Desmond said, unsuccessfully trying to push past Luke. "I was leaving."

"I think you should stay," Luke said. He wore jeans that showed off his toned thighs and a long sleeve t-shirt that was half a size too small.

I averted my eyes.

I was taken, and he was leaving.

Desmond huffed and walked back into the office.

"I'll tell you the same thing I told Rylie—this case needs to be left to the professionals—the police."

"The same police who failed to solve the case the first time?" Desmond crossed his arms over his chest.

Luke kept a friendly but serious expression on his face. "We did everything we could. And we will do everything we can this time too."

"We?" I couldn't keep my mouth closed any longer. "Aren't you leaving the country in a few days?"

Desmond scowled at Luke. "You won't even be here to work on the case? Who are you to tell us to stay out of it?"

"Someone who won't be here to cover for the two of you if you decide to go ahead with this rogue investigation."

I don't know what infuriated me more—Luke acting like he was doing something to protect me or the fact that he was acting like a pompous jerk. I'd helped him with three other cases, but I wasn't qualified to do anything on this one?

"I don't know what threats you've made against her," Desmond said. "But I'm not backing down, regardless of how much you threaten me."

"I didn't threaten anyone." Luke turned to me. "Is someone threatening you?"

"No," I said. It was pointless telling him what Detective Bryant said, especially since he seemed to have some sort of love affair with the guy.

"Any more words of warning? Or am I free to leave?" Desmond asked.

"Go ahead." Luke stepped away from the door and further into the office. "But keep your nose out of this. It will only end badly."

"I don't know if there's anything worse than not

knowing what happened to my sister," Desmond said then turned to me. "I'll text you."

As Luke and I watched him leave, something stirred inside me. I didn't care how badly Luke and Shayla wanted to keep me out of this. It wasn't fair. They were pushing this guy out when all he wanted to do was find his sister. If my sister went missing, I sure as hell wouldn't let some cops intimidate me. I'd do everything I could to find out what happened to her.

"Please don't tell me you're considering working this case with that guy?" Luke said.

I snapped the lid on my empty spaghetti container. "So what if I am?"

Luke tipped his head back and studied the ceiling of the office. "You're impossible."

"Yep. Unprofessional too, apparently."

"I wasn't trying to say you're unprofessional. You're just not trained as a police officer."

"That didn't stop me from helping on the last three cases."

"How many times did you almost die because of your involvement with these cases?"

"Twice," I said.

"And both of those times, you were dealing with amateur murderers."

"Are you saying the guy who killed Selena is a professional?"

"From the looks of things, yes." Luke shoved his hands in his pockets. "And I don't want to call home in a month and find out you were his next victim."

"Why do you think Selena is dead? Maybe she's just being held against her will."

Luke looked torn like he needed to convince me to stay out of the investigation, but to do that, he'd have to give me more information.

"Finding a prosthetic arm and a shoe hardly qualifies as a reason to believe someone is dead," I continued. "And there were absolutely no clues in the original case other than her being missing."

"No clues that were public knowledge," Luke said. "There were plenty of clues. They suggested not only was Selena murdered, but she was murdered brutally."

"Do you think it was the husband?"

"No way to know," Luke said, not meeting my eye.

That was a yes.

"What I know is that I don't want to end up hearing you've disappeared in the same manner. And consider how shaken Shayla would be if she had to work her best friend's murder case. It's just not worth it."

"But if he's done it, isn't it even more important that we—sorry—you," I said when he gave me an irritated expression, "put this guy behind bars?"

"Just because we suspect someone of doing it—not that we suspect Jacob, but if we did, it doesn't mean we're right. And someone as powerful as Jacob Marquez likely wasn't the one who got his hands dirty, so to speak."

"You think someone did this for him?"

Luke shrugged.

"Cedric hates Jacob."

"Now, you're on a first-name basis with two of the

suspects?" He rubbed a hand over the stubble growing on his chin. "Actually, three."

"Three?"

"Desmond."

"Desmond said he'd been cleared," I said. "He had an alibi."

"And he knows you have no way to confirm that. He knows the cops won't talk to you. He knows you're in just as much of a pickle as he is. If you think he's not danger-ous, you didn't read the news stories from the initial investigation."

He was right. I hadn't really kept up with the story. "I hardly think that mouse of a man could have killed Selena and lived to tell the story."

"Underestimating him because of his size is a rookie mistake. Sometimes the smallest people are the strongest and most dangerous."

I didn't respond.

"I love that you care enough to try to get justice for Selena. But there is an entire police department that wants justice too."

"Does it, though? What if he paid them off?" I reached into my pocket and felt for the check. "He has enough money. His business almost went under during the initial investigation. I'm betting he'd do just about anything to keep his name clean."

"Please, Rylie. I'm begging you. Stop." Luke's voice was pleading. "You're going to get in over your head on this one. Nothing is as it seems. It's like there are optical illusions all around us. Do you want to know why Detec-tive Bryant is so worked up about this case?"

"Because he's a—"

"Rylie." Luke's tone was the same one that my mother had when she heard me cuss.

I crossed my arms over my chest and looked out the window.

"He's the one who had the case initially. He's the one who followed all the clues only to turn up empty-handed."

"I just want to help," I said. "I wouldn't be in the way."

"I know you think that, but you don't know how far-reaching your actions can be. Think of Shayla's career. I'm established within the department. They couldn't let me go because I was associated with you, but Shayla isn't. They could fire her if they think she's helping you."

"I'd never ask her to do that." Even though I had asked her for information that morning. I was a terrible friend. "I don't want her to lose her job."

"Then quit while you're ahead. You haven't done anything yet that could get either of you into trouble, have you?"

I thought about my conversations with Cedric and Jacob that morning. Of the check in my pocket. Of my interactions with Desmond. "I don't think so."

"Good."

He seemed to think that was the final word about me working on the investigation. And I let him.

"I'm guessing you're still angry that I'm leaving?"

"Why wouldn't I be? You have a good life here, and you're leaving to save money for a house?" I shook my head. "It makes no sense."

"Saving money for a house is only one factor," he said. "I need a change of scenery."

"He needs to get away from me," Nikki said as she walked into the office, Antonio following close behind. "Though this is the first time a guy has fled the country to escape my reaches."

Luke opened his mouth as if he might say something, then snapped it shut.

My drama meter was about filled for the day. "What's up, Nikki? Antonio?"

"I wanted to give you an update on the kids," she said. "You know, the ones who are doing everything they possibly can to get both of us fired."

"I think I'll head out," Luke said.

Nikki didn't respond. She just stood there with her hands resting on her duty belt. Antonio kept his eyes glued to the floor.

"Okay, bye," I said.

But Luke was too focused on Nikki to hear me. When he realized she wasn't going to say anything, he let himself out of the office.

"That was mean," I said.

"Me? I'm the mean one? *He* broke up with *me* to leave for two years." She plopped down on the stool behind the counter. Antonio pulled out his phone, ignoring us. "If he thinks I'll wait for him, he's got another thing coming."

I highly doubted he expected her to wait for him, but I wasn't about to tell her that.

"Two years is a long time," I said. "But maybe this is for the best. A few weeks ago, you said he was boring you."

She didn't seem to appreciate the reminder. "That's not what I'm here to talk about." She glanced at Antonio, who seemed wholly unfazed by our conversation. And I couldn't help but notice he looked like he'd been working out extra hard. His biceps bulged from beneath his long-sleeved uniform shirt.

"Earth to Rylie," Nikki said.

Antonio looked up and caught me staring at him. I averted my eyes down to my hands.

"I came to tell you how you're going to keep your job." Nikki sounded exasperated.

"What would make you think I'm going to lose my job?" Had she been talking to Detective Bryant?

"Because you led ten tweenagers on a mountain lion hunt that led to a missing woman's appendage."

"When you say it like that it sounds pretty bad," I said. "But I knew they weren't mountain lion tracks. And the appendage was a prosthetic. It's not like they found a mutilated corpse."

Nikki held up a hand as if disgusted by my excuses. "Thankfully, none of that matters to the judge."

My stomach soured.

"Even with all the parental objections, the judge recognized that the likelihood of another instance like this happening is slight. They'll be back to complete their community service hours."

"Seriously?" My voice came out whinier than a tweenager's who'd just had their phone taken away. "There's so much going on with the case right now."

"I don't know what that has to do with the community

service group." Nikki looked down at her perfectly mani-cured nails. "The trail is open."

"If I may." Antonio's voice startled me. "What I believe Rylie is trying to say is that *she* may be busy with the case."

Nikki looked at him as if he had grown another head. "Rylie has been told to stay out of this case."

Antonio shrugged and returned to looking out the window.

"You are staying out of it, right?"

When I didn't immediately answer, Nikki threw her hands in the air. "If you want to be a cop, go be a cop."

"I don't want to be a cop," I said.

Antonio grunted but didn't turn around.

"I really don't. But I think there's more to this case than meets the eye. And I want justice for Selena."

"You can be really stupid sometimes. You know that?" Nikki said. "Look, I don't care what you do on your own time. But when you're here, you'll be supervising the kids. Got it?"

I mumbled an okay.

"Just don't get yourself in trouble, going all rogue. You have no idea how much Luke did to protect you." Nikki's eyes misted over. "It drove me crazy."

"I'm sorry," I said, patting her awkwardly on the shoulder. "You'll be okay."

"Easy for you to say. You have guys falling all over themselves to marry you."

I glanced at Antonio, but he didn't even flinch.

She didn't know about the kiss between Antonio and me. Though she and I had become something like friends over the past few months, I still didn't trust her completely.

"Guys are not falling all over themselves," I said. "Trust me."

"That ring you keep in your pocket begs to differ."

A blush warmed my neck. Antonio's gaze flickered to my hand.

"This is not about me," I said, trying to change the subject. "I know it sucks that Luke is leaving. I'm sad too. But maybe there's a reason for all of this. Maybe there's a different guy who is better for you than Luke—a guy who you would have never met if Luke stayed."

She was quiet for a moment. "Just be ready for those kids. And stay out of trouble."

esmond hadn't texted me the entire day, and by the time I was heading home, I figured things had fallen through with the private investigator.

When I walked through the door of my apartment, I came face to face with an angry-looking Shayla.

"What's up?" I asked. "Did Fizzy chew up your work boots again? I'm really sor—"

"Fizzy didn't do anything wrong. You did." I hadn't heard her this angry in a long time.

"What do you mean I did?" Did she know about me talking to Desmond? Or Jacob and Cedric?

"You think I don't know that you already knew about Luke the other night. Why didn't you tell me? Prepare me so I didn't make a huge fool of myself?"

"It wasn't my story to tell," I said. "I'm sorry."

"I can't believe he's leaving. Just leaving. As if no one even matters." Tears hung in the corners of her eyes.

"I know. I'm sad too."

"If anyone can make him stay, you can."

I laughed. "Me? Luke doesn't care what I think."

"You can't honestly believe that. He still lo—"

The smoke alarm cut off her words.

"The cookies!" Shayla ran into the kitchen.

Smoke billowed from the oven as Shayla tried to pull the cookie tray out.

I yanked the fire extinguisher from the wall and aimed the hose at the oven.

"Are they on fire?" I shouted over the alarm.

"Not yet." She threw the charred cookies into the sink and turned on the water. "I can't believe I burned them."

"Seriously, Shay, what's going on?" I replaced the extinguisher, pulled out the broom, and started swatting at the air in front of the smoke alarm to get it to shut up.

"Nothing's going on other than Luke is leaving, and you didn't tell me."

"I only found out an hour before you did."

We were still shouting. My waving wasn't helping in the slightest.

"Plus," I continued. "You've been baking and cooking for weeks. There's more to this than Luke leaving."

"Maybe it's that my best friend has gone rogue, my TO hates me, my mother thinks I'm a failure, and Seamus is going to *propose*."

"What do you mean, Seamus is going to propose?" I yelled.

"He asked me to go to Ireland with him. There's only one reason he'd ask me to go to Ireland."

"To meet his family?" I was now beating the actual smoke alarm with the broom.

"And to propose." She stared down at the charred remains of the cookies.

"Is that really so bad?"

"I can't get married. I'm too young to get married. And then he'll want kids and I'll have to quit my job and be a stay-at-home mom and get fat again and—"

"Whoa, whoa, whoa," I said. "Slow down. No one said anything about kids and being a stay-at-home mom, right? I'm sure that's not what Seamus wants."

"His mom stayed home with him."

"That doesn't mean he wants the same from his wife."

Shayla paled at the word wife.

"Denver Fire, we're coming in," a voice shouted from the door.

Three firefighters in full bunker gear, air tanks, and masks barged into the kitchen, holding a hose and a fire extinguisher.

"Don't spray," I shouted. "There's no fire. Just a stupid alarm that doesn't know when to shut up."

Eli Hudson—Quarterback for the Denver Broncos and our landlord's son—walked in behind the firefighters. "What happened?" He asked.

A tiny brunette in a Broncos hoodie and jeans stood next to him with her hands on her hips.

"I was trying to make cookies," Shayla said.

The alarm still blared. My head was starting to pound.

"I'll call the alarm company and tell them to shut it off," Eli said. He left the room, but the woman stayed behind, evaluating the situation.

Within minutes, the alarm quit, and the room went eerily silent though my ears still buzzed.

"Thank you for coming," Shayla said to the firefighters as they left.

"And you are?" I asked the woman.

"Logan Labrec." She held out a tiny hand and shook mine with more gusto than most men. "Eli's girlfriend."

She was not what I'd expect him to choose as a girlfriend. The man was absolutely gorgeous, and this woman was—well—ordinary. Plain. She couldn't have been any taller than five foot two and probably weighed a hundred pounds soaking wet. Her long dark hair was pulled back into a tight ponytail, and she wore no makeup at all.

"That's the reaction I usually get," she said with a laugh.

I realized both Shayla and I had been overtly sizing her up.

"She's more than she seems," Eli said, walking back in and slipping an arm behind her back. She barely came up to his armpit. "This girl's going places. She could have easily been the first professional female quarterback, but she'd rather be a sportscaster."

Logan smiled up at him. "And I'm doing it without anyone's help."

"That's great," Shayla said. She hadn't ever been that taken by Eli since she wasn't a huge football fan. "I'd offer you a cookie, but I burned them all. I think I have some cake left from the other night though. And I can put on a pot of coffee."

Eli shrugged, and Logan smiled. "Sure, we'll stay."

As they made their way to the kitchen talking about Logan's career in broadcasting, my phone vibrated. The screen showed Desmond's name.

"I'll be right there," I said, but Shayla wasn't paying me any attention. "Hello?" I said into the phone.

"I need your help. He's trying to kill me." Desmond was out of breath, fear coursing through his words.

"Who's trying to kill you?" My pulse quickened. Why would he call me? Why not the police? "The private investigator?"

"Not the P.I. Jacob. He's in his SUV. He keeps ramming into my car."

A loud bang came from the other end of the line.

Desmond screamed.

"You need to call the police," I said. "Desmond?"

"I'm here," he finally said, his voice weaker than before. "The police don't care about me. They won't help. Jacob will just pay to have this pushed under the rug too. Whatever happens, please do not call the police."

"Where are you?" I asked, not making any promises.

"I'm outside the gate to Shadow Trail."

"Why are you there?"

"I was going to text you so we could meet," he said. "I had something I needed to show—oh God, he's getting out of his car."

"Drive away," I whisper yelled.

"I can't the airbag's deployed."

"Then get out and run."

On the other end, I heard a car door open and shut, and Desmond's breaths coming faster and harder.

He was running.

I should have ended the call and dialed 9-1-1.

The sound of chain-link came through the line as if he was climbing the fence. But the eight-foot chain-link fence was topped with circles of barbed wire. He'd never get over it.

"Desmond, don't climb the fence," I said. "Run."

Desmond didn't respond. There was no way he could climb the fence and hold a phone. He had to have put it down.

Silence fell over the line for what seemed like forever before a single gunshot rang out, leaving me temporarily deaf in one ear.

11

I pushed my phone up to my good ear, trying desperately to hear something.

Anything.

"Desmond?" I whispered, knowing he wouldn't respond.

It was as if the line had gone dead. I disconnected the call and typed in nine, one, and then stopped.

What if Desmond was right. What if I told them he was there and then Jacob paid to have it all brushed under the rug? He'd begged me not to call the police.

I had to get out there to see if I could help. Maybe the gunshot had missed him. Or maybe Desmond got the gun away from Jacob.

If I got there and it was a murder scene, I'd call the police.

Anonymously.

I tried not to imagine the worst.

"Who was that?" Shayla asked, making me almost topple over the back of the couch.

"It was—um—Garrett. He wants me to come over tonight."

"You should have some cake first," Logan said, taking a huge bite and closing her eyes in bliss. "This is delicious."

There's no way I could focus on cake when a man could have just been murdered.

"I don't want any cake." My words were sharper than I intended. "I mean, I had some the other night. Anyway, I need to go."

"Is everything okay with you and Garrett?" Shayla whispered so only I could hear. "Have you started making wedding plans?"

"Everything is fine. Good. We're good. We'll make them soon." I pulled my jacket off the hook and opened the door.

"Are you going to take Fizzy?" Shayla asked.

Fizzy.

Where was Fizzy?

"He's probably hiding from the smoke alarm. Do you mind if I leave him? He'll be too freaked out to get in the car."

"I don't mind at all," Shayla said. "Let me know if you need anything."

Worry was written all over her face. I should have just come clean. Told her what I'd heard. But she'd go to her TO or worse, Detective Bryant. Then she could be in trouble because I was involved. I couldn't risk it until I knew what was going on.

When I pulled up to the gate of the reservoir, there wasn't any indication that a car had been rammed over and over again. Not a single bit of bumper or headlight.

Nothing.

Had it happened here? Or was Desmond mistaken?

I parked Cherry Anne across the road behind a group of bushes and walked across the street. One lone street lamp flickered at the entrance gate.

If what Desmond had described had happened here, it was likely someone had seen and called the police. Before going into the reservoir, I dialed Desmond's number. If I found his phone, I'd know this was the place.

It took three rings before I saw a small light in the tall grass about ten feet from the gate.

My stomach dropped.

Part of me hoped I wouldn't find it. Finding it meant Desmond had been here and was likely inside the reservoir. Possibly dead.

But if there was any chance he was alive, I needed to get in there and help him.

I pocketed the cell phone, unlocked the gate, and slipped inside. I'd call the police the minute I knew what was going on.

The light from the gate didn't shine very far into the parking lot, but it didn't need to. The moment my eyes adjusted to the partial darkness, Desmond's body came into view.

It looked like he was napping.

There was no blood.

I held my breath, hoping for the best.

I pushed my fingers to Desmond's neck but felt no pulse.

I pushed harder.

Nothing.

Desmond was dead.

One gunshot wound to the chest, and he'd crumpled into a pile on the ground.

I took a step back.

I didn't want to disturb the crime scene, or leave any evidence that I'd been here, but clutched in Desmond's right hand was a piece of paper I might have missed entirely if it hadn't been for its neon green color and the first three letters of my name peeking out.

Carefully, I slipped the paper out of his hand and shoved it in my pocket with his phone.

Why hadn't the killer taken it from him? They had to have seen it.

With one final look at the man who had only wanted justice for his estranged sister, I turned and left the park.

Once safely back in my car, I opened the note and read.

Go to my house (201 W. Branch Street) the code is 4456. My board will give you all the information you need. Thank you for your help. —D

Great. Now I had to help. Not that I wasn't going to, but it was a dying man's last wish.

I estimated I'd have ample time to search Desmond's

house if I called the police anonymously on my way over. The phone Desmond had dropped was a burner phone, and the only number programmed into it was mine. I erased my contact information and all correspondence we'd had and then dialed 9-1-1.

"9-1-1, what's your emergency?" a man's voice answered.

I tried to make my voice sound high pitched and annoyed. "I think I heard a gunshot at Shadow Trail Reservoir."

"A gunshot at Shadow Trail Reservoir?" the man confirmed. "And who am I speaking with?"

I hung up the phone, turned it off, wiped it down to remove my prints, and threw it out the window into the bushes I was parked behind.

The police would be here for hours processing the crime scene. It was highly unlikely they'd get to Desmond's house before tomorrow.

I had plenty of time.

I put on a pair of gloves, punched the code on the number pad above Desmond's door handle, and slipped inside. The smell of cat urine hit my nose and made my eyes water almost as bad as when I'd done my pepper spray training. I pulled my shirt up to cover my mouth and nose and made my way through the piles of garbage stacked all around.

This guy was a verifiable hoarder.

It wasn't hard to find the board since the house was especially tiny with only one bedroom, one bathroom, and a small kitchen and living room. In the bedroom, a board covered an entire wall. Multi-colored strings weaved their way around push pins holding pictures and scribbled notes.

There was no way I would be able to read everything before the police arrived. Upon closer examination, all the strings led to one man.

Jacob.

I rubbed my head. The smell was giving me a

headache. I snapped a couple of pictures of the board with my phone and decided to take another quick look around.

Carefully, I stepped around piles of old newspapers and magazines that had gone out of print years ago. Boxes of broken toys sat in one corner of the bedroom. The closet door was partially off its tracks with clothing spilling out.

Just as I was about to leave the bedroom, a crash came from the hallway.

I flattened myself on the floor between the wall and the bed and waited.

Had the police gotten here already? Or was it someone else? Someone who needed to cover his tracks.

If Jacob found me snooping around, he'd surely kill me too. I should have cashed his check and given the money to charity, at least.

The house was dead quiet. As if someone was waiting for me to show myself.

The carpet smelled like a mixture of cat pee and cigarette ash. I'd definitely have to wash my clothes when I got home.

If I got home.

A tap at my heel nearly made me scream.

I turned slowly to find a tabby cat rubbing against my shoe. I sighed a breath of relief. The noise had probably been from the cat knocking over a stack of magazines.

To be safe, I waited a bit longer. The bed was messy with its sheets askew and stained pillowcases, but the floor underneath the bed looked a whole lot worse.

I opened my phone so the screen could provide a tiny

bit of light. If someone came to the doorway, they wouldn't be able to see it.

Moldy fast-food and candy bar wrappers, toenail clippings, and underwear that had been long forgotten made me want to gag. But when the light of my phone flashed on something shiny and red, I paused.

The house was still silent. I was almost certain no one was there.

Thankful I was already wearing gloves, I pulled out a shoe that matched one I hadn't seen long before. At the reservoir.

This shoe belonged to Selena.

It was the one she'd worn to her gala the night she'd gone missing.

And it was under Desmond's bed.

I pushed the shoe back into its original position, took a photo with my phone, and stood up. I needed to get out of there. Luke was right. Desmond was the killer. The shoe proved it.

Jacob probably found out Desmond killed Selena, so he killed Desmond out of revenge.

But then what was the purpose of Desmond putting the board together? Was it to frame Jacob?

I didn't have time to think of possibilities now. I snapped a couple more pictures and decided not to push my luck.

I'd parked a few blocks over in case Luke or Shayla were assigned to search Desmond's house. They'd instantly recognize Cherry Anne, and I'd never hear the end of it.

A knock at the door nearly made me fall over a pile of clothes. This time it definitely wasn't a cat.

"Police. Is anyone home," a man's voice said.

He sounded tired, not like he was about to break down the door. I tip-toed toward the back of the house and prayed the police weren't covering the door that led to the alley. When I peeked through the crusty dust-filled curtains, I couldn't see anyone.

"Police," the voice said again. "We're here to follow up on your call. Open the door." His voice was more forceful now.

If Desmond had called the police, why didn't he tell them Jacob was trying to kill him? And why didn't he stay on the line and lead them to the reservoir?

Something was off.

But I didn't have time to think about it. If the police found me in Desmond's house, I'd definitely lose my job. Heck, they might even think *I* killed Desmond.

I turned the handle quietly and slipped out onto the concrete step. The fresh air was a welcome sensation in my lungs.

When the door closed silently, I let out a breath of relief.

I took a step onto the ground, but it was much softer than what the frozen grass should have been.

In a split second, I found out why.

A screeching meeeoooowww rang out through the neighborhood. A Siamese cat hissed and swatted at me as I took my foot off its tail.

"Someone's out back," I heard the man's voice say from inside the house. How they'd gotten in without making any noise was beyond me. Maybe they had the code too. Or maybe I hadn't re-locked the door.

I sprinted as fast as I could toward the back of the lot. Thankfully, Desmond didn't have a fence. When I heard the officer yell at the cat to move, I was around the corner and out of sight. I made it to Cherry Anne, fired her up, and drove away as quickly as I could without drawing suspicion.

I headed in the direction away from Shadow Trail.

Being nearly midnight, I didn't want to go to Garrett's house. And if I went back to the apartment, Shayla would give me the third degree. That only left one place.

My parents' house.

13

It took the entire thirty-minute drive to calm my nerves. I snuck into the basement to the room I'd lived in before Shayla and I had gotten our apartment.

The bed was like a pair of open arms welcoming me into its folds. I stripped off my disgusting clothes and dove under the sheets. I wanted to look through the pictures more thoroughly from Desmond's house, but I couldn't keep my eyes open.

The smell of bacon and coffee brought a smile to my face long before the sun came up. My soiled clothes from the night before were clean and neatly folded on the chair next to the door.

"Good morning," my mom said when I got to the top of the stairs. I'd taken a shower and tied my wet hair up into a messy bun.

"Hi," I said. "Thanks for washing my clothes. Sorry if I woke you when I came in."

"If anything woke me, it was the stench on those

clothes. Why in the world did you smell like a pile of garbage?"

"It's a long story," I said. And not one I was about to get into with her.

"I didn't expect you. I hope the sheets were okay."

"They were perfect." I slipped a slice of bacon into my mouth and closed my eyes. It was moments like these I missed being at home.

"Don't eat all the bacon, it's for your father," Mom said.

Then again, living on my own had its advantages.

"I can throw the sheets into the wash before I leave. I'm off today anyway."

"Don't worry about it. They were getting musty after not being used for so long." Her guilt-trip game was on point today. "Have you enjoyed your freedom from my clutches?"

"It's been okay. I mean, I've missed seeing you every day," I added for good measure. "But living with Shayla is nice."

"I bet she's much cleaner than you are."

I raised my eyebrows and took a sip from the cup of coffee she'd just poured for me.

"What? It's no secret that you're rather messy. How does Garrett feel about that?"

"He has a housekeeper." I shrugged.

"I guess he'll be able to save money when the two of you are married, then."

"How's that?" The thought of being married twisted my stomach with anxiety. The last time I'd lived with a man, I'd found him naked in our bed with another woman.

"He can let his maid go. That's the job of a wife."

Maybe in her house, it was.

"We'll probably keep her on. It's not like saying 'I do' will instantly make me into a clean freak."

Mom gave me a look of irritation but didn't push. "Speaking of Garrett, when are we going to work on wedding plans? I mean, I have a whole binder of ideas. And I went to the bookstore and got some wedding magazines. You're welcome to wear my dress. I think Megan still has it from her wedding. But what about a venue?"

My eye started to twitch. I had not had enough coffee for this discussion. "Garrett and I haven't really had a chance to talk about the wedding much."

"Is he still mad at you for kissing that Italian man?"

Mom never was one to have any sort of filter. "We're working through it."

"That's good. Because if he hadn't forgiven you, he shouldn't have given you that ring." She grabbed my hand. "It's so beautiful." She pulled my hand closer. "Is that blood?"

I yanked my hand away and examined the ring. Sure enough, there was a speck of blood on the band. It had to be Desmond's. I thought I'd been careful.

"It's probably just ketchup," I said, walking to the sink to wash the blood off.

"You've been working on another case, haven't you?"

She couldn't possibly know that. "What case would I be working on?"

"The Selena Marquez case. I saw you in the background of the press conference with her husband and his floozy."

"You mean his wife?" I asked.

"Elodie is not Jacob's wife." She spoke as if she knew these people. "I'm sure she'd like to be, but Jacob refuses to marry her."

"How do you know all of this?"

"I read the magazines in the check-out aisle."

I sighed. "You know those aren't real, right? Like, they lie about everything."

"Not about Jacob and Elodie. I know a lady who does prenatal yoga with Elodie, and she said Elodie's always complaining about how Jacob is still in love with Selena."

"So you don't think Jacob is responsible for Selena's disappearance?"

Mom narrowed her eyes. "I knew it. You *are* investigating this."

"I'm not investigating anything. I'm just asking what you think. I think someone other than Jacob killed Selena and disposed of her body where no one will ever find it."

"Like at Shadow Trail Reservoir?"

"Maybe. What's your theory?"

"I think Elodie killed her." Mom took a sip of coffee.

"Why would Elodie have killed her? Did she even know Selena before all of this?"

"Elodie was Jacob's assistant for years. They were having an affair."

If that was true, I needed to refocus my efforts. Was there a link between Elodie and Desmond? Could they have killed Selena together?

"What about Selena's brother?" I asked.

"The creepy one?" Mom nodded. "He could have done it, but I thought they said he had an alibi."

"Do you remember what it was?"

"Something sketchy. Like drugs or hookers or something."

Desmond didn't seem like the drug or hooker type to me. But it had been a while ago. "Thanks for the coffee and clean clothes. I need to run."

"Aren't you forgetting something?" Mom asked.

I hesitated for a minute. My ring was on my finger. My phone was in my pocket . . . my pocket. The note and the check.

I looked up to find my mother holding both as if she had a winning hand of cards.

"I can explain," I said.

"Explain why you have a check for $100,000 from a possible murderer?"

"I thought you said you thought Elodie—"

"And the address to a man's house who was involved with hookers and drugs?"

"How did you know it was his address?"

She frowned. "I know how to use the Google."

Rolling my eyes would not help the situation, but it was so hard not to.

"Please stay out of the investigation. Let Luke handle this one."

"Luke is moving to the Middle East next week," I said, hoping to distract her.

"What?" Mom's eyes widened. "He can't leave."

"You can tell him that." I carefully pulled the check and the note from her hand and deposited them in my jacket pocket. "Thanks again for the clothes and breakfast."

But she wasn't listening. She already had her phone in her hand typing frantically. I couldn't help but smile at the thought of her letting Luke have it.

14

I got in position just before Shadow Trail was scheduled to open to the public. I laid flat on my stomach in the tall grass on a hill just north of the gate with a pair of binoculars.

From what I could tell, the police were still in the parking area, a tent covering where I'd found Desmond the night before.

Mixed emotions poured through me. Part of me wanted to cry after getting Desmond's call and seeing his lifeless body. But the other part of me was almost certain he was responsible for Selena's disappearance.

How else would he have had the shoe?

But there was also the Elodie angle. Did she want to get rid of Selena so she could have Jacob all to herself?

The sight of Antonio opening the gate caught me by surprise. I hadn't realized he was the one scheduled to open the reservoir today.

As if on cue, Jacob Marquez jogged into sight and

flashed his annual pass at Antonio before he stopped dead in his tracks at the sight of the tent.

He turned to Antonio, probably to inquire about what was going on. Antonio shook his head.

If he had truly been responsible for killing Desmond, would he have shown up at the crime scene? Probably, if for nothing else but to keep up appearances.

But the way Jacob moved around the tent as he made his way to the trail, didn't look like someone who knew what was going on. Like someone who had killed another human in cold blood.

I needed to talk to Antonio. See what Jacob had said to him.

But how would I do that without looking suspicious? I wasn't supposed to be working the case. And if word got to Garrett that I'd shown up early when I wasn't even on the schedule to see Antonio, he'd probably take the ring back.

Antonio disappeared into the ranger office, and I decided to take a chance.

I dialed the office number on my cell.

"Shadow Trail Reservoir Ranger Station, how can I help you?" His silky Italian voice made my breath catch.

"Antonio?" I managed to squeak out.

"Yes, who is this?"

I cleared my throat. "Sorry, it's Rylie."

"Rylie?" he said my name slowly as if he couldn't quite believe I'd be calling.

"Uh, yeah, it's me. Sorry to bother you. If you're busy, I can call back later."

"You are never a bother to me." He paused. "What do you need?"

"This is going to sound crazy." How could I ask him about Jacob? He would know I was spying on him.

"You want information about the dead body?"

"How did you—"

"I could ask the same of you. I know the news hasn't picked up the story yet, but I don't really want to know how you already knew someone had been killed here. Unlike a beautiful blonde shit magnet I know, I like to keep my nose out of police business."

His flirting was a jolt to the system after he'd barely spoken to me since we'd kissed. "I, uh—"

"It's Selena's brother, Desmond."

"Do you know how he died?" I asked.

"Gunshot. The police were already here when I got here to open, but I know one of the guys, and he gave me an overview."

"Did Jacob show up to run the trail?"

"Yes," he said slowly. "Why?"

"If anyone were going to kill Desmond, it would probably be the guy he has a restraining order against, don't you think?" I was proud of myself for coming up with such a good explanation on the fly.

"You think Jacob killed this guy and then showed up to run at the murder scene the next day?"

"If he hadn't shown up, it would have been weird. He's there every single morning."

"I don't know. He seemed confused by the whole thing."

"Did you tell him who died?" I asked.

"Of course not."

"Did he say anything to you?"

"Nothing out of the ordinary. But I should tell the police he's here if you think he would be a prime suspect."

"No," I yelled into the phone. I glanced around to make sure no one heard my outburst, but I was still completely alone on the hill.

"Why not?"

"Because they'll know you talked to me. It's not widely known that Desmond has a restraining order against Jacob, but *Detective Bryant*," I couldn't help but say his name with disgust, "talked about the restraining order in front of me."

"There could be a killer in the park as we speak, and you don't want me to tell the police just because they might put together that you called and talked to me?"

"I don't think you're in any danger. If I did, I'd say go for it. But my job could be in jeopardy. I could go to jail if Bryant finds out I'm poking around."

"What do you have against Harry?" Antonio asked.

"Who's Harry?"

"Harry Bryant. He's a good guy."

"Don't tell me you're friends."

"And what if we are?" His flirtatious voice had vanished.

"Never mind. Forget you ever heard from me this morning. And please, if you tell your buddy Bryant that Jacob's in the park, don't bring me into it."

"I would never want to do anything to hurt you." His voice softened. "But I do think I should tell Harry about

Jacob. Just to be on the safe side. I won't say anything about you, though."

"Fine. I should go. Have a good day."

"It was nice talking to you. I couldn't say anything with Nikki around, but congratulations on your engagement."

"He knows what happened Christmas Eve," I blurted out.

"I wondered if you'd told him. I guess it's good you were honest."

"It kind of slipped out. And I may have ruined Christmas."

"I'm sorry. It should have never happened in the first place."

"Are you apologizing because you wished it wouldn't have happened?" Why did I ask that? What did it matter if he regretted kissing me? Was my pride so easily damaged?

"I don't regret it. I had wanted to kiss you since the moment I first saw you. But I knew you were involved with someone. It was wrong of me. I hope you will forgive me and we can go back to being friends."

"Of course," I said, though I didn't feel like I needed to forgive him. The person I needed to forgive was myself. "Talk to you later."

"Bye," he said.

I hung up and stared at my phone. I needed to get my heart in check. Antonio wasn't my fiancé. I didn't love Antonio. I loved Garrett. I was going to marry Garrett. Antonio was just a handsome man who showed me attention. And I was just nervous about getting married. Who wouldn't be? Marriage was a big commitment. But Garrett was the man I would marry. The man I wanted to marry. End of story.

And I wouldn't even get started on Luke.

I peeked through the binoculars again to see Antonio talking to Detective Bryant.

It irked me to see them chatting like old friends. I needed to get home and spend some time with Fizzy. Take him on a walk and let the police handle this investigation.

They'd figure out eventually that Jacob killed Desmond, and Desmond killed Selena. They didn't need my help.

I stood and turned only to run straight into a sweaty, angry-looking man.

Jacob.

Before I could scream, Jacob had one hand over my mouth and the other around my torso, holding my arms at my sides.

"Trust me," he whispered. "You do not want to alert the police that I'm here."

The tone of his voice was dangerous. I tried to get the pepper spray on my hip, but of course, it wasn't there. I wasn't in uniform.

"Stop fighting," he said.

Yeah, right. I tried to wiggle free, but he was unusually strong for a man his size.

The only thing I could think to do was gross, but I had to try. I opened my mouth and licked his hand like my nephews did to each other.

The trick worked. He released me. "That's disgusting. Why would you lick me?"

I didn't answer his question.

I ran.

The last time I'd run so hard was my final high school track meet. I'd won first place in the four hundred.

But it was apparent I was no longer a runner.

Jacob caught me easily just before I reached Cherry Anne. This time, though, I could defend myself.

I turned and aimed a punch at his nose.

He ducked, but I still caught him in the forehead.

"Rylie, stop," he said, holding up his hands. "I'm not going to hurt you."

"You killed Desmond. How do I know you won't kill me too?"

"I didn't kill Desmond. Wait," his eyes widened. "Desmond's dead?"

I kept my fists raised, but my guard dropped slightly. "Don't act like you don't know. That's why the police are at the reservoir."

All the color drained from his face, and his eyes glazed over with tears.

He really hadn't known about Desmond.

At that moment, a big black Escalade flew into the parking lot and stopped inches before hitting Cherry Anne.

Cedric burst from the driver door, aiming a gun at me.

I threw my arms in the air.

"What are you doing, Cedric?" Jacob said. "Put the damned gun away."

Cedric hesitated. "She attacked you."

"After I attacked her," he said, then turned to me. "Unintentionally. I'm sorry I snuck up on you. I just didn't want you to yell and draw the cops' attention."

I looked from Jacob to Cedric, who still had a gun pointed at me.

"Put. The. Gun. Down." Jacob's voice was furious.

Cedric did as he was told.

"Let's get in the car, and we can talk," Jacob said, motioning to his SUV.

"Uh, no thanks. We have nothing to talk about." Even if he hadn't killed Desmond, I still didn't want to be in a car with him and his gun-waving lunatic of a security guard.

I unlocked Cherry Anne and slid into the driver's seat. The car was hot from the sun, and I was sweating from running. I yanked my jacket off and threw it in the backseat.

"Fine," Jacob said, "then I'll come with you. Cedric won't even follow us."

Cedric looked like he wanted to object.

"It'll be fine," Jacob said to the both of us.

"Okay, get in," I said. "But only one lap around the block."

"Good." As Jacob hurried around to the other side of the car, I pushed the record button on my phone and dropped it into the cupholder in the center console. "Now, tell me about Desmond," he said when he closed the car door.

I put the car in reverse and came as close as I could to Cedric without making contact, then drove out of the parking lot. "First, I have a question for you."

"Okay," he said.

"Is that Escalade the same one Cedric always drives?"

Jacob looked behind us at the car. "Yes. It has his license plates."

"Do you own any other vehicles like it?"

"I have a deal with the Cadillac dealership. I have about five of them on lease."

"Do you know if any of them incurred any damage recently?" As in last night, I thought.

"Not that I'm aware of. Why?"

"No reason."

He waited, then moved on. "Now can you tell me about Desmond?"

"There's nothing else to tell. Desmond is dead."

"And why do you think I killed him?"

I couldn't tell him that Desmond called me right before he'd been shot. "He has a restraining order against you. I figured it was the most logical thing. Plus, what else would you do when you found out he killed Selena—the wife you are still in love with?"

Jacob stared out the windshield. He had a good poker face. It probably served him well in business.

Finally, he spoke. "I do still love Selena. That's the truth. But Desmond didn't kill her. And even if he had, I wouldn't have killed him. I've changed a lot over the past few years."

"How so?" I asked. "You stopped beating your wives?"

He clenched and unclenched his fists and took a deep breath. I was treading on thin ice, but I had to get him to talk.

"Among other things, yes."

I couldn't believe he admitted to beating his wife.

"Technically, Elodie is not my wife."

"I heard," I said.

"But I've never laid a hand on her in anger," he said. "I don't know what happened to Selena—I didn't kill her—but I know ultimately it was my fault."

"Why do you say that?"

He sucked in a breath. "The night she went missing, we had an argument."

"At the gala?"

"Before. At home."

"What about?"

"Extramarital affairs," he said. He was holding his words close to his chest.

"Elodie?"

"Among others," he said. "That's not what's important. What's important is that I lost my temper. I slapped her across the face. If you look at the photographs from that night, you can see one cheek is redder than the other. She was already so frail after all those cancer treatments. It was the first time I hit her since she'd been diagnosed. Then, she was gone."

"Do you think she left on her own accord?"

He shook his head. "I wish that was the case."

"How can you be sure it's not?"

"The police found blood—a lot of blood—Selena's blood—in the car."

"Was Cedric driving?"

He ran a hand through his hair. "I wish he had been. But no. I forbade it. I kept him for myself."

"Who was driving? Maybe they're responsible."

"When I wouldn't allow Cedric to take her, Selena drove herself." Tears were now making paths down his cheeks. "If I had just gone with her like we'd planned. Let Cedric drive us. She'd still be here—alive—probably not with me, but alive."

I drove more slowly. "Where did you go that night?"

"I'm not proud of it, but I went to see Elodie."

"Elodie was your alibi?"

He nodded. "And Cedric, and the hotel management where we stayed."

"Where were you last night?" I asked.

"In bed. Elodie, Cedric, the housekeeping staff can all attest to that. I took a sleeping pill at seven o'clock and didn't wake up until this morning when I went on my morning run."

If Jacob hadn't killed Desmond, who had?

My bets were on Cedric. He was the one wielding the pistol this morning and seemed only too happy to shoot me in the light of day. Plus, he's the one who drove the SUVs.

"Do you think Cedric could have killed Desmond?"

Jacob shook his head slowly. "I don't think so."

"You don't sound sure."

"Cedric knows that if he steps out of line, he'll be punished."

"By you?" I asked. "I thought you were a changed man."

"Not by me. Cedric has a duty to the family. The same as I do."

"The family? Like the same family?"

"Why is that so surprising?"

"There's just not much family resemblance."

"Because we don't have the same skin color?"

I shrugged.

"Did you decide to cash the check?" Jacob asked.

"No."

"As in no, you're not going to cash it, or no, you haven't decided?"

"Both? Neither? I don't know."

"Just cash it," he said. "You could probably use the money."

Of course, I could. I could pay off Cherry Anne and my student loans and have some left over. I could go into my marriage debt-free. But at what cost? "I'll think about it," I said.

As we approached the parking lot, there was no sign of Cedric. Instead, there were four police cars.

"Did you call the police?" Jacob asked.

"You've been with me the entire time."

"Then how did they find me?"

"It's not like you were hiding. You ran right past them this morning."

Detective Bryant shook his head when he saw Jacob with me. "Why can't you stay out of things?" he asked when I stepped out of the car.

Two other officers met Jacob at the door. "Jacob Marquez, you're under arrest for the murder of Desmond Pratt and Selena Marquez."

"You can't arrest me," Jacob said. "Talk to Elodie. She knows. I was home."

But he wasn't directing his words at Detective Bryant.

He was directing them at me.

Jacob's face was that of terror as they loaded him into the back of the police cruiser.

"He didn't do it," I said.

"You can tell us everything down at the station," Detective Bryant said.

I looked at him for a moment. "I'm not going to the station with you." I needed to talk to Elodie. To clear Jacob's name and see if she had any idea who might have killed Desmond and Selena.

"You don't have a choice," Bryant said. "You're under arrest."

"For what?" I took a step back.

"Interfering with an investigation." He stepped toward me. "I warned you. Don't make this harder than it has to be."

He pulled a pair of cuffs from his belt.

For a moment, I wanted to resist. Run. But he would have caught me. And I really didn't want him messing up my favorite pair of jeans. I offered my wrists, and he snapped the cuffs on behind my back.

The cold metal of the cuffs rubbed on my wrist bones, making my temper flare.

I didn't hear a word of the Miranda Warning Bryant was rattling off. My mind raced with thoughts of how disappointed Shayla would be and how Jacob was innocent and how I needed to talk to Elodie.

They put me in an interrogation room when we got to the station. It was better than a cell, but I still wasn't free to go. At least I wasn't wearing the handcuffs anymore.

When the door opened after what seemed like forever, Detective Bryant, Shayla, and her TO walked in.

Shayla's eyes were slightly red. She had been crying but had done a good job of covering it up. Only someone who knew her well would be able to tell—a friend. Though, I wasn't sure if she'd still consider me her friend after this.

"Would you like to explain why you don't think Jacob is responsible for the two murders?" Detective Bryant said as he sat in the chair across from me. Shayla and her TO stood behind him.

"Would you like to explain to me why you think he is?" I asked.

"You think this is a game? You've been arrested. You could go to jail. You'll probably lose your job. Especially if you don't cooperate."

"I don't think it's a game, but I also don't think you

have enough evidence to convict Jacob of the murders. If you did, you would have locked him up when Selena first went missing."

"Maybe we've come upon additional information."

"Like the arm and the shoe?"

"Among other things," he said.

Was he talking about the board in Desmond's house? I hadn't had an opportunity to look through the pictures on my phone.

"Jacob has an alibi for both nights," I said.

"You and Jacob seem to be good friends." Bryant leaned back in his chair. "Maybe you helped him kill Desmond."

Shayla stifled a gasp.

I gaped at him. Then panic welled up inside me. If they searched my car and found the check, they'd surely think the only reason I was defending Jacob was because he'd bribed me.

"Don't look so surprised." He ignored Shayla. "We know Desmond was harassing you. Texting and calling and showing up at your place of work."

"He wasn't *harassing* me. He was trying to get me to help him find Selena."

"You mean find her killer?"

Damn. "Yeah, I mean her killer."

He narrowed his eyes at me. "Did Desmond think she was still alive?"

"Who knows what he thought," I said as airily as I could. "He was kind of crazy. But I didn't kill him."

"Where were you last night?" Bryant asked.

"I was at our apartment," I said, looking at Shayla.

"And then I was going to go to my boyfriend's house, but I went to my parents' house instead."

Shayla frowned. Did she know I never had any intention of going to Garrett's house?

"Did you go straight to your parents' house?"

"Yep," I lied. "You can ask my mom. She knows I was there."

"We already have."

If mom told them what time I got there, they'd know I lied. But by the look on Bryant's face, she hadn't.

"What would you think if I told you Jacob's alibis have fallen through?"

"What do you mean, they've fallen through?" I asked.

"Elodie admitted she lied."

"If she wasn't with Jacob, does *she* have alibis for those nights?"

I was just throwing it out there, but the way Detective Bryant's mouth twitched told me he hadn't thought of this angle. Though I'm sure he would have gotten there.

"From what I hear, Elodie was only one piece of Jacob's alibi," I said. "Cedric can probably attest to where he was last night and maybe even the night of Selena's disappearance."

"Cedric has conveniently gone missing."

"Then maybe he did it," I said. "Maybe he killed them. I mean, he *is* the one who drives the Escalade."

"Why would that matter?" Detective Bryant asked. "From what we know, Selena drove herself the night she was murdered—and yes—she was murdered. We may not have found a body, but no one could lose that much blood and live."

"I guess you're right." I shrugged, thankful he hadn't caught onto me knowing about Cedric's car bashing into Desmond's. Especially since they probably hadn't found Desmond's car yet.

"Do you know why Desmond was at the reservoir when he was killed? Or how he got there?"

He still thought I had something to do with all this.

"If I give you the information I have, will you let me go?" I asked.

"If I let you go, will you stop looking into this investigation?"

I didn't answer. We sat staring each other down. I could see Shayla shift from one foot to another out of the corner of my eye.

Finally, Detective Bryant spoke. "I cannot give you permission to continue with this investigation."

I didn't respond.

"But I do want to know what you have. Let's say, if it's good enough, I'll let you go."

"That doesn't seem very fair," I said.

"It doesn't have to be fair. I could lock you up for interfering with an investigation after being given multiple warnings not to do so."

I considered this. I'd never be able to speak to Elodie if I was stuck in jail. "Okay, I'll tell you what I have."

He smiled. Shayla looked irritated but relieved. Her TO looked like an asshole.

"You saw the arm and the shoe. We both did."

He nodded.

"But I've spoken to Jacob multiple times. He jogs at the reservoir every day. And he's never acted out of sorts."

"Maybe he's just a good actor."

"Or maybe he didn't do it. I mean, today, he jogged right past the tent covering Desmond's body without flinching."

"You weren't working this morning. How do you know that?"

I raised my eyebrows.

"Antonio told you, didn't he?"

"No," I said too quickly.

Shayla's eyes narrowed.

"But you did talk to him this morning."

He knew.

"I did."

Shayla shook her head and looked down at her shoes.

"But it was because I wanted to know if Jacob said anything to him."

"And?"

"He didn't. He had no idea."

"And did Antonio tell you it was Desmond?"

I didn't want to get Antonio in trouble, but I couldn't admit that I already knew. "Yes. But when I told Jacob, he was genuinely surprised and seemed almost sad."

"What else did he tell you on your little joyride?"

This guy was getting on my nerves. "Nothing you probably don't already know."

"Try me."

"He told me about the night Selena disappeared."

Detective Bryant's mouth twitched again. "And what exactly did he tell you?"

"If you let me go, I'll let you listen for yourself."

"You have a recording?"

I nodded.

He hesitated.

"Okay," he finally said. "But if it's not good enough information, you'll be right back here."

"Deal."

Shayla and her TO stayed at the station while Bryant took me back to my car.

"I hear you're pretty torn up about Luke leaving," he said.

"He's a friend," I said, trying not to give up my true feelings.

"We're all bummed by it too."

Was he trying to be my friend now? Did he think that would make me want to give him more information?

"You know, if you wanted to become an officer, you'd probably be a good one."

"Thanks, but I don't."

"Why not?"

"Because I don't want to carry a gun. I don't want to go on annoying calls. I'm not cop material."

He laughed. "So you figure you'll just take the fun parts?"

"I like to see justice served." I shrugged. "And I don't feel like justice has been served for Selena."

He mumbled something under his breath.

"What's really going on with this case?" I asked. "Did Jacob pay off the department to keep quiet?"

"If he had, do you think he'd be in a jail cell right now?"

"Then why did this case get pushed under the rug?"

"You know I can't tell you that."

I narrowed my eyes at him. "Do you even know?"

"Here we are," he said, pulling into the parking lot where I'd parked Cherry Anne. I gasped at the sight. Her windows had been bashed in, the trunk was open, and the tires were flat.

"What the hell happened here?" Detective Bryant asked.

I turned an accusing eye on him.

"You and I both know the police wouldn't do this to someone's car."

"Then who did?" I snarled.

"We'll find out."

I got out of the police car and carefully walked around the car.

"Don't touch anything," Detective Bryant said. "There might be prints."

I wasn't about to touch anything. When I got to the other side, a shiver ran down my spine.

The word STOP was spelled out in green spray paint that looked terrible against the red door.

"You're gonna want to see this," I said.

Detective Bryant came around the other side and frowned.

"Now do you think I'm responsible for Desmond's murder?"

"I never thought you were," he said. "That looks like a threat."

"Stop what?" I asked.

"Investigating. We found a similar note at Desmond's house."

"What else did you find at Desmond's house?" I asked, trying not to let on that I knew more than I should have.

"We're still going through all of it. It was a disaster." He looked inside the car. "It looks like they didn't take anything."

My work bag was still in the trunk, though all the contents were spilled out. My uniform shirt, duty belt, and bulletproof vest hadn't been touched at all. My purse was on the floorboard of the passenger seat, while everything that was inside now littered the mat. And my phone was in the cupholder exactly as I'd left it.

"I never turned off the recording," I said, reaching through the window careful not to cut myself on the shards of broken glass, and picked up the phone.

"You shouldn't touch that."

"Don't you want to hear what's on it?"

He hesitated then nodded. "Play it."

17

The first part of the recording was basically what I remembered.

"Why were you asking about his cars?" Detective Bryant asked.

"I had a hunch."

"What kind of hunch?"

I didn't respond. I wasn't about to give away that Desmond had called me and told me he was being rammed by a car like the one Cedric drove.

The rest of the conversation elicited very little reaction from Detective Bryant. He took a few notes when Jacob talked about the night Selena had died.

When we heard Detective Bryant arresting me, he didn't look my way.

Then the recording was quiet.

The entire recording was four hours long.

We listened for a bit, but nothing came through. My patience was wearing thin. I fast-forwarded.

"What if we miss something?" Bryant asked.

"I don't want to sit here for four hours listening to this with you. I can send you the recording, and you can listen to the entire thing yourself."

I fast-forwarded some more. Still nothing.

"I will want you to send it to me."

I fast-forwarded again and landed directly in the middle of what sounded like my windows being smashed in.

"Rewind it," Bryant said.

I glared at him.

"Sorry. I just want to know what happened."

"I do too," I said and rewound it until it was silent again. Then we waited.

Finally, we heard what sounded like a car approaching—a loud car. The engine idled as we heard two doors slam shut.

Almost instantaneously, we heard the windows shatter, one by one. The sound brought tears to my eyes. Cherry Anne was almost like a member of my family.

"Do you see it?" A woman's voice said.

Bryant looked at me expectantly.

I shrugged, my palms up. How was I supposed to know what they were looking for?

"It's not here," a man who sounded a bit like Cedric said. "Maybe he never gave it to her."

Bryant looked at me expectantly. I shrugged. I had no idea what they were talking about.

"Open the trunk," the woman said.

A shuffling to unlock the door and open the trunk, then a click. The voices became muffled, but it sounded like the two people were arguing.

We listened as they presumably dumped out my work bag. Thankfully they hadn't taken my duty belt or badge. Not that having a park ranger badge would get them very far.

The woman's voice was the next thing we heard. "It's not here."

"Maybe she doesn't have it," the man's voice said.

"If she does, she could ruin everything."

My mind reeled. What would I have that was worth breaking into my car for?

"Just leave the message, and let's get out of here before someone sees us," she said.

"Do I have to?" the man asked.

"Should I grab that pepper spray from the back?" she said, then laughed.

"That's not even funny," he said, but his voice wasn't angry. They actually sounded like they were pretty chummy.

And now I knew the man was Cedric.

The faint sound of a spray paint can came and then stopped.

"And flatten the tires for good measure."

"You want me to slash her tires?" Cedric sounded taken aback.

"No. Don't slash them. Just let out the air. It's already going to cost her a fortune replacing the windows and paint."

Yeah it was.

I remembered the check in the pocket of my jacket in my backseat. I'd probably have to cash it now.

On the recording, we could hear the car doors close again and the car driving away.

There was still over an hour left on the recording, but the rest of it probably didn't matter.

"Mind telling me what happened there?"

The only thing I knew for sure was that the man was Cedric. Otherwise, I was as clueless as he was. "I wish I knew," I said. "Maybe they got the wrong Mustang."

The look he gave me said he and I both knew that wasn't the case.

"Either way, doesn't this prove it wasn't Jacob? I mean, he was in custody when all of this happened."

"What makes you think whoever did this is the same person who killed Desmond and Selena?"

"Didn't you say Desmond got the same note as I did? Wouldn't that mean—"

"That you could be next?" Bryant gave me a pointed look. I hadn't thought of it that way.

"Did you recognize the voices?" he asked.

I shook my head. "Did you?"

"I have a hunch, but I'm not entirely sure."

"Care to share?" I asked.

"Why would I share when you refuse to do the same?"

"I know nothing," I said, but we both knew I was lying.

"This is why I didn't want you on the case in the first place. I know you know something. You can keep telling yourself you're in it to find justice, but you can't fool me. You're either doing this because you like the thrill of the chase or because you like the attention you get when you solve a crime."

I opened my mouth to refute his accusations, but he cut me off.

"Just send me the recording." He handed me his business card with his cell written on the back. "Do you need a ride somewhere? We're going to have to process this like a crime scene."

"I'll call my boyfriend," I said. "I mean, fiancé." I looked down at the ring. I still wasn't used to calling him my fiancé.

When he was distracted calling the crime scene techs, I pulled my jacket from the backseat. The check and the note were still inside the pocket. I transferred them to my jeans pocket before asking Detective Bryant, "Can I take my jacket with me? I'm a bit chilled."

He glanced over and shook his head, motioning for me to put it back, then returned to his phone call.

I put it back and wrapped my arms around my torso. It wasn't a particularly cold day, but all the adrenaline in my body had dissipated. Chills ran up and down my arms.

18

My car was already being processed by the time Garrett showed up.

"Sorry, babe. I got here as quickly as I could." He looked over at my car. "Holy cow. What's this all about?"

"It's nothing," I said, instantly regretting asking him to come pick me up. I should have called my sister or Nikki. This would just make Garrett more worried than he already was.

"It doesn't look like nothing. It looks like you could be in danger."

"Give me one second," I said and walked back over to the trunk of my car. "Can I take my uniform stuff for work?"

I had asked the guy processing the items, but Detective Bryant cut in. "You won't be needing them."

"What?"

"You've been suspended." He held out a printed email

from Ursula Vilago, the Parks and Recreation Director. My big boss.

"And here I thought we were bonding."

"I didn't get you fired. That should count for something."

"When do I get un-suspended?" I asked.

"That depends on your actions," he said.

I knew he wasn't talking about how quickly I could solve the crimes.

"Once I'm confident you won't interfere anymore, I'll ask the director to reinstate you."

"They can't suspend me on your word alone."

"Even if Ursula and I weren't personal friends, your arrest today sealed the deal."

I let out a frustrated growl. "How am I supposed to pay my bills?"

"Not my problem," he said and turned away from me.

"You can't take anything that was in the car when this happened," the crime scene technician said.

"I got that," I said, my voice angry.

I probably should have put my phone back, but there was no way I would give them my phone loaded with incriminating evidence. Thankfully, I'd already gotten the check and the note.

I got into Garrett's car without a word.

"Did I hear him say you're suspended from your job and that you got *arrested* today?"

"He's just being a prick," I said. "I did nothing wrong."

"Didn't he tell you not to intrude?"

I glared at Garrett.

"Sorry," he said.

I looked back at the road.

"How about we go on a date tonight? It's been a while since we've been out together, just the two of us." He reached across the center console and grabbed my hand, rubbing a thumb over the diamond ring. "I miss you."

My frustrations slipped away. "I miss you too."

"Then it's settled." His smile could melt the polar ice cap. "I'll take you home so you can get ready. I'll go to my last meeting, then I'll pick you up at seven."

"Sounds like a plan," I said.

That would give me time to go through the photos on my phone.

He dropped me off at my apartment with a kiss.

"I love you," he said as I stepped out of the car.

"I love you too," I said. I still felt like a middle schooler when I told him I loved him.

When I got to my apartment door, I was about to slip the key inside the lock, but I could hear Shayla on the other side speaking loudly with someone—presumably on the phone, because I could only hear her side of the conversation.

"Yes, we all think it was Jacob," she said. "No. Cedric is not a suspect." She paused. "Because he's not."

She didn't think Cedric could have done it? Maybe she didn't know about the gun he carried.

"I know about the loose dirt. How do *you* know about the loose dirt?"

Loose dirt? Was that a police metaphor?

"Of course, they would tell you. You're not even on the force anymore, and you're still getting information."

Ah, she was speaking with her mother. Probably the

only person she'd speak to about the case who wasn't on the force.

"Look, I have to go." There was a pause. "I know what's on the line. I've been briefed."

I almost fell over when Shayla threw open the door.

"Hey," she said, dropping her phone to her side. She was holding Fizzy's leash with a very excited dog at the end. "How long have you been out here?"

"I just got here," I said. "Why?"

She looked down at her phone. "No reason."

Guilt settled deep in my stomach. "I can take Fizzy."

"Why don't we go together?" she asked. "Then you can tell me about your car."

I bristled at the fact that she didn't want to give me any information, but she wanted me to spill everything to her.

"Sorry I had to be in the room while you were being questioned," she said as we made our way down the block. Fizzy hopped along happily next to us, stopping at almost every tree to mark his territory. "They thought if you saw a familiar face, you'd tell them what you know."

"It's okay," I said. "I wasn't upset with you."

"Can I ask you a question?"

I shrugged. "Sure."

"Please don't get mad, I just want to know."

That didn't sound good. "Okay."

"Do you think maybe you're throwing yourself into this case because you're trying to avoid what's happening in your own life?"

Her words hit me like a ton of bricks. "What do you mean? What's going on in my own life?"

"I mean the whole thing with you and Garrett. I know it hasn't been easy picking up the pieces after Christmas."

"We're doing fine," I said. "He's forgiven me, and we're moving forward."

"Have you set a wedding date?"

My eye twitched. "Not yet. We haven't had a lot of time to work on wedding plans."

"Exactly my point," Shayla said. Her voice was gentle, but her words grated on my nerves. "You've made yourself pretty busy with Selena's case. Do you think maybe subconsciously you're doing it to escape your own issues?"

"No. I'm doing it because the police can't get their shit together and solve this damn case. Selena deserves better. She had a shit life growing up, a shit life with Jacob and the cancer, and then she ends up murdered and no one but her brother—who is now dead too—seems to give a damn."

We walked in silence for a while, my words hanging in the air like a blanket of smog.

"I hear your car is in bad shape," she finally said.

"I almost cried."

"Why do you think they targeted you?"

"They were looking for something."

She stopped and studied me. "How do you know?"

"I got a recording of the entire thing."

"How did you get a recording? Did you know something like this might happen?"

"No." My voice sounded way more defensive than necessary. "I had the recording going when Jacob was in the car with me."

"Did you give the recording to Detective Bryant?"

"He listened to it with me. And then I sent it to him."

"Good." She began walking again. "What do you think they were looking for?"

"Beats me."

I'd gone through it a dozen times in my mind since I'd heard the recording. But there wasn't anything related to this case that I would have had in my car. Other than the photos on my phone and the check.

"Maybe it was just a random break-in?"

"It was definitely related. Bryant said Desmond had a similar note in his house as the one they left for me."

"They left you a note?"

We both stopped to let Fizzy do his number two.

"More of a message. In spray paint."

"What did it say?"

"It just said stop."

"And what did Desmond's say?"

I gave her a look.

"Detective Bryant probably didn't tell you, right?"

"He hasn't told me anything." Fizzy finished his business, and I picked it up with a poop bag. "And he gets mad at *me* for not being a team player."

"To be fair, he doesn't have to be a team player. You're not really on the team."

"Exactly," I said, my bitterness seeping out. "But if he doesn't have to be a team player, then neither do I." I knew I sounded like a child, but I couldn't help it.

"Aren't you even a little bit worried that what happened to Desmond could happen to you?"

"Why should I be?" I turned and headed back toward

the apartment. Shayla followed. "If the police are right, they've locked up Desmond's killer."

"But Jacob couldn't have done those things to your car. He was already in custody."

"You're right. He was. So do you—do the police—think more than one person wanted to kill Desmond?"

"I think more than one person was angry with Desmond. Probably for different reasons, though."

"Why would anyone want him to stop looking into Selena's disappearance if they weren't the killer?"

Shayla pondered this for a moment. "Just because Jacob didn't destroy your car himself, doesn't mean he wasn't responsible."

"That might be true," I said. "But I still don't think Jacob's responsible for Selena's murder. Not directly, anyway."

"What do you mean, not directly?"

I pulled out my phone and played the recording.

"So he was abusive," Shayla said. "Desmond was right."

"You talked to Desmond?" We walked up the stairs to the apartment.

"He came to the station once or twice. Trying to make his case mostly. He thought Jacob did it." She unlocked the door. "Maybe Desmond was right about that too. Maybe Jacob did kill Selena, and when Jacob found out Desmond knew, he killed Desmond to shut him up."

"But Desmond didn't think Selena was dead."

"Maybe not when you talked to him, but some of the evidence we found in his apartment indicates differently."

There had to be more on the board than I'd initially seen.

"What about Cedric?" I unsnapped Fizzy's leash, and he did his crazy run around the apartment. "Why doesn't anyone think he's a suspect? He did pull a gun on me this morning. Maybe he shot Desmond."

"Cedric pulled a gun on you?" She looked at me, horrified.

"He thought I was attacking Jacob, but Jacob was attacking me." I waved a hand. "It's nothing. We sorted it out. But Cedric did have a gun."

"We haven't been able to find Cedric," Shayla said. "He's been MIA since we took Jacob into custody."

"Maybe the family killed him."

"What family?"

"His family—Jacob's family. They're related, you know."

Shayla frowned. "I don't know that I did."

"Cedric mentioned it in passing." I shrugged. "He said he couldn't let anything happen to Jacob or else."

"Or else what?"

"I don't know, but it didn't sound good."

Shayla pulled off her shoes and hung her coat on the pegs by the door. "You know, if you have something that would clear Jacob's name, you should turn it in to the police."

The problem was, the only information I had was a gut feeling and a shoe under a dead man's bed.

19

I went through the pictures of Desmond's board over and over again and didn't find much that meant anything to me.

Photographs of Cedric, Jacob, and Elodie were all connected by red strings to one of Selena. From the looks of things, Desmond believed they were all suspects, but Jacob's name was circled five times in red marker. Whether that meant he thought Jacob killed Selena was beyond me.

He had also circled a few words: Shadow Trail Reservoir, Florida, and Gala.

Obviously, Shadow Trail was where the arm and shoe were found. And Gala was where she was headed the night she disappeared. But Florida? What was that about?

I'd looked at the photos so many times my eyes were starting to cross. The one the police most needed to see was the one of the shoe under the bed. There was something about the shoe that didn't settle right with me.

Maybe it was that it was the main piece of evidence

that could clear Jacob and make Desmond the prime suspect in Selena's murder. But if I gave it away, the police would know the depth of my interference.

They'd find it eventually and come to the same conclusion I had.

When the doorbell rang, I realized I'd spent my entire afternoon going over the case. I was starting to feel as crazy as Desmond and was getting just about as far as he had.

"You're wearing the same clothes you were earlier," Garrett said, glancing at my dirty jeans and t-shirt. I ran a hand over my ponytailed hair to smooth down the fly-aways.

Garrett, on the other hand, looked smoking hot. He had gelled his hair and trimmed up his beard. His outfit—dark gray slacks and a light blue button-down under a light gray sweater and a dark blue sport coat—probably cost more than one of my car payments. Just the thought of Cherry Anne brought tears to my eyes.

"Don't cry," he said, pulling me in for a hug. "I didn't mean you don't look beautiful. You do. We're just going somewhere a bit fancier tonight. If that's okay, I mean. If you don't want to, we can go wherever you want."

I pulled back. "I'll go change. Give me ten minutes."

Garrett looked at his watch. "We will still be able to make our reservations."

I left him in the living room with Fizzy and ran back to my bedroom.

The disappointment on Garrett's face when he saw me unprepared for our date made my heart ache. I was letting him down. Maybe Shayla was right. Maybe I was using this case to distract me. I needed to give Garrett more of my attention. I wasn't getting anywhere with the case anyway.

I reached into the back of my closet and pulled out my sexiest little black dress. It was an off the shoulder, three quarter sleeved mini-dress that hugged my curves in all the right places. I wrapped my hair into a chignon and added about three pounds of mascara. For a final touch, I put in the earrings Garrett had gotten me for our six-month anniversary.

Next to the earrings in my jewelry box was a necklace I had only worn once even though it was beautiful.

I could have worn it. The tiny Denver Broncos logo surrounded by what I assumed were fake diamonds—though they sparkled like real ones—would have finished the outfit with a tiny bit of classy flair. Garrett wouldn't know it had been a gift from Antonio. But I did. And it felt wrong.

I closed the lid on the necklace and checked to make sure I looked okay in the mirror hung on the wall. I slipped on a pair of black heels and did my sexiest walk out of my bedroom, spinning in front of where Garrett sat on the couch.

"Damn, you're hot," he said, standing. "Maybe we should just stay in."

I looked at the time. "Ten minutes on the dot. We better head out so we don't miss our reservations."

I grabbed Garrett's hand and pulled him out the door before I gave in to his attempts at keeping me in the house. Not that I would have minded if it weren't for my growling stomach.

"Have you thought much about the wedding," Garrett asked? "We should probably decide on a date, at least."

"We will," I said, the twitch in my eye returning. "I'm sorry I've just been distracted."

"I know. You must really care about Selena to go to such lengths to find her killer."

It was like he could finally see me. "I do care. I don't know why, but I do."

"Your ability to care so deeply for people is one of your most endearing qualities."

I smiled. "Thanks, babe."

"So about that wedding date? What do you think about this summer? We could even have it on a beach somewhere."

This summer was so close. "I don't know that I'd have enough time to plan something so quickly."

"Fall then? The trees are so pretty in the mountains when they change color."

"But you can't plan a wedding on the trees. There's usually only one or two good weekends, and they're completely dependent upon the weather. Miss it by one week, and you have bare brown trees. Not so pretty."

He laughed. "Winter then?"

I had nothing—no reason to refute winter. Honestly, I'd always thought I'd get married in the winter. "Winter might work," I finally said.

He squeezed my hand. "You'd make a beautiful winter bride."

Thankfully, we arrived at one of the newest and fanciest Italian restaurants in Denver.

"Lisa from work had nothing but good things to say about this place."

I frowned. I'd never heard him talk about specific women from work. Something about another woman giving him ideas on where to take me on a date left a bitter taste in my mouth.

"She came here with her husband," he said, noticing my silence.

"I don't care. I mean, I know you work with women." I laughed nervously.

He walked around to the other side of the car and opened my door for me. "You have nothing to worry about." He looked me up and down.

I smiled and laced my arm through his to steady myself on my heels. The weather was starting to warm up, which meant mud. My shoes might not have been designer like Selena's, but I still didn't want to have to scrape dried mud off them.

I shook my head to clear my thoughts. I wasn't going to worry about the case tonight.

"You okay?" Garrett asked.

"I'm great." I squeezed his arm. "I'm glad we get to have a date tonight."

"Me too."

The restaurant was so packed it was hard to get to the hostess station.

"I'll go tell them we're here for our reservations," Garrett said with a smile.

I stayed back and watched the people around me. Couples huddled close. Groups of friends laughed.

I checked my phone. Not that I was about to hear from

anyone. A pang shot through me knowing that Desmond would never text me—or anyone else—ever again.

No.

I couldn't think about that. I needed to be fully present for Garrett. He deserved my attention. And I had to prove to myself that I wasn't using the case to put distance between us.

"Hey babe," Garrett said from behind me. "I want to introduce you to someone."

I turned to find Garrett standing next to Cedric.

"This is Cedric Kinney," Garret said. "My college roommate."

I hesitated. Cedric hesitated.

Neither of us was going to make a move.

He was one of the people responsible for killing Cherry Anne and possibly two humans as well. He had pulled a gun on me less than twenty-four hours ago.

But Garrett knew none of this. And when I met his eye, he looked confused by the standoff.

"It's a pleasure to meet you." I gathered up all my nerve and held a hand out. "Cedric, was it?"

Cedric clutched my hand. "I've heard so much about you, Rylie."

I pulled my hand away and resisted the urge to rub Cedric's murderous germs onto my dress. "You two talk a lot then, huh?"

"All the time," Garrett said.

"Funny," I said. "I've never heard you talk about a Cedric."

Garrett looked at Cedric apologetically. "That's because we called him Ace."

"This is Ace?" I asked. As in the guy who got top honors in accounting? The guy Garrett practically idolized?

Cedric stood a bit taller. He didn't look like an accountant.

"The one and only," Garrett said.

"Are you still an accountant?" I asked.

"Yep," Cedric said. "I work for a non-profit called Neleas." His glare dared me to mention his other job. Obviously, Garrett didn't know this was the guy who did Jacob Marquez's dirty work. Had he known who I was all along?

"Never heard of it," I said with a shrug.

"That's because they're primarily based in Florida," Garrett said.

My gaze leaped from Garrett to Cedric.

Florida?

Cedric looked confused and shifted his huge takeout bag from one hand to the other.

Florida was one of the words Desmond had circled on his board. Could this be the link?

"Oh, there's our buzzer," Garrett said, oblivious to the fact that he might have just solved part of a murder case for me. "It was great seeing you, Ace."

"You too," Cedric said.

"We'll have to have you over when you're back in town."

Cedric winced. So, he was going out of town? Probably to Florida. I'd have to ask Garrett later.

"That sounds like fun," Cedric said, then turned and walked out of the restaurant.

"Please follow me," the hostess said when Garrett handed her the buzzer.

"You said he's headed out of town. Is he going to Florida?" I asked, trying to keep my tone neutral.

"Yeah, he goes every month. Has to check on some things with the non-profit."

We sat at a cozy little booth in the back where the noise level was significantly quieter than in the lobby.

"What kind of non-profit is it?"

"It's a shelter for battered women," he said. "A friend of his was killed at the hands of her husband, so he set it up to honor her."

Sounded like a familiar story.

"And that's his full-time job?" I asked. "How does he make money doing that?"

"His full-time job is as an accountant," Garrett said. "Why the interest?"

"Just intrigued, I guess. I've always wondered how people make money running non-profits."

"They have donors. People leave money to them in their wills. That kind of stuff. I'd guess he gets a salary, not that he needs it." Garrett was looking at his menu, trying to decide on what to eat.

"What do you mean? Is he from a wealthy family?"

"Something like that." He turned the page to the entrees. "He was always tight-lipped about it. Like he didn't want to be treated differently than anyone else. For all I know, he could be related to the Queen."

I laughed. Cedric could not be related to the Queen. He was a murderer. He told his friends that Jacob killed his wife without using Jacob's name.

Or maybe Jacob *had* killed Selena, and I had it all wrong. Either way, I needed to know more about Neleas. Maybe it was some sort of shell company. Maybe it—

"Earth to Rylie." Garrett waved his hand in front of my face with a laugh. "You okay?"

"Yeah," I said with a smile.

"Good. What are you going to have for dinner?" He nudged the menu toward me. "I hear the fish is to die for."

I opened the menu and took a peek. I definitely didn't want fish. "I think the gnocchi sounds good."

"Gnocchi sounds delicious."

"This week has been crazy, and some comfort food seems like it might be just the trick."

"I saw on the news before I came over that the police arrested Jacob Marquez for the murders of Selena and Desmond."

"You did?" I asked. I hadn't realized it had gone public.

"You don't look happy," he said. "I thought this was a good thing. It meant the case was over."

"My car was destroyed *after* they took Jacob into custody," I said.

"So you think—"

"It was someone else."

He ran a hand down the side of his face. "And you're not going to give up until you know, are you?"

I shrugged. I didn't want to get into this.

"Either way," he said. "I ordered you a rental car. I'm sure your insurance will pay for it, but if not, I can. It should be delivered to your apartment by tomorrow morning."

My heart swelled. "Thank you. You didn't have to do that."

He reached across the table and grabbed my hand. "I do have to do that. You may think you have to save the world, but you're my world, and I want to be your hero."

His words brought tears to my eyes. After everything with Antonio and investigating these crazy cases, he still wanted me—wanted to be my hero.

"Can I get you something to drink?" the waitress asked, shattering our love bubble.

"I'd like a beer," I said. "Any beer."

"I'll take a margarita," Garrett said. "And I think we're ready to order as well. I'll take the fish, please."

"And I would like the gnocchi," I said.

"Good choice," the waitress said to me. "We're famous for our gnocchi."

"How's work?" I asked when the waitress had gone. Garrett was one of the lead accountants for the Denver Broncos. "I feel like it's been a while since we've talked about how life is going with you."

"Work is fine. Busy as usual. I got box seats for us at the home opener."

"What?" I nearly jumped out of my seat. "You can't just say that as if it's nothing."

"I wanted to surprise you."

"You definitely surprised me." I could have squealed, but the restaurant was too fancy for that. "I can't believe we're going to be sitting in box seats."

"I guess I've been doing well lately, so they gave me a bonus. I had my choice of this or cash. I figured you'd like this better."

He chose to watch a Broncos game over cash? Even though he worked for the Broncos, he wasn't the biggest football fan.

"Thank you."

"You're welcome." He smiled like he had on our second date. The date he later told me was when he knew he was in love with me.

After Garrett dropped me off at my apartment, I changed back into my jeans, a black hoodie, and boots, and called an Uber to pick me up.

I needed to speak with Elodie. I was almost one hundred percent sure Cedric had taken her dinner, and if he told her about me knowing about Florida, she might leave.

On the way, I Googled Neleas.

It looked legit. There was no mention of Selena by name, but her story was told in a roundabout way. If Cedric headed all of this up, he must have cared for Selena. And if he found out that Desmond was responsible for Selena's murder, he might have gone after Desmond. But how did Elodie fit? Why would she be involved in anything that glorified her husband's ex?

Either way, Cedric was on my do-not-mess-with list. He was the one who put the warning on my car. And he was the reason I stopped at the sporting goods store on my way to pick up a can of bear spray.

When the driver approached the Marquez residence, I realized going there might have been a mistake. News crews sat idly in their vans—cameras pointed at the gates. If I tried to go in, they'd record every second. It already sucked enough that I was suspended from my job, but I didn't want it to become permanent.

"Can you take me around the block?" I asked.

The driver waved a tattooed hand as if she didn't care.

We drove around the block. Fences separated the houses in the back. To get to the back door of the Marquez house, I'd have to sneak into another person's yard and climb the fence.

"You can leave me here. Thanks."

She stopped the car, and I got out. The house that backed up to the Marquez's was completely dark. Hopefully, that meant they were either gone or in a deep sleep.

I did my best to be quiet as I made my way up the driveway. The gate wasn't even closed. I let out a sigh of relief.

Now, I just had to get through the yard and over the fence.

But as I stepped through the gate, a motion detection light turned on, blinding me momentarily.

A dog inside the house started barking. It sounded big.

Without thinking, I took off running across the back yard. Toys were all over the place, some partially buried in the snow.

I was mere feet from the fence when I heard them let the dog out.

The barking grew louder and more vicious.

I was almost to the fence.

The Marquez's mansion was in full view.

Then my foot twisted in a hole beneath the snow.

The frozen ground was unforgiving.

I went down hard.

The dog was too close. It was going to bite me.

I tried to stand, but my leg gave out. I silently hoped for a twist and not a break.

The dog was on me now.

His teeth bare.

I pulled out the can of bear spray and pointed it at the dog. Just as I was about to hit the trigger, the dog started humping my stuck leg.

"You've got to be kidding me," I whispered. "Get off me."

The dog—a sheepdog—didn't care what I had to say.

I tried to stand up again, and this time was nearly successful, but the dog had its legs wrapped around my stuck leg.

I plopped back on my butt. I couldn't shoot the dog with bear spray when he wasn't hurting me. I shoved it back in my pocket.

Voices shouted for the dog as a flashlight beam landed on us.

I stood up—ignoring the pain—and pulled myself over the fence.

"Stop," a male voice said from the yard with the dog. "I'm calling the police."

Yeah, like that would make me want to stop.

I turned and hobbled toward the Marquez house.

I had no idea what I might say to Elodie when I

reached the house, or if I'd even make it inside, but I had to try.

The man from the other yard was now at the fence, shining his flashlight my way. I pulled the hood over my hair and kept run-limping.

Motion sensor lights didn't come on. Even when I was so near the house, I could smell what they'd had for dinner—fish.

I was almost to the door when the ground fell out from beneath me.

My nose filled with water. Ice cold water.

I tried to swim, but my jeans and hoodie were saturated, pulling me down.

Another light hit my face as I got to the surface and took a breath.

"Don't move," a man said, pointing a flashlight and a gun at my face.

I didn't have a choice. I was back under water.

A strong hand grabbed the hood of my sweatshirt and pulled me to the surface.

"Let go of me," I screamed. It was a good thing the neighbor had called the cops.

"Shut your mouth," the man whispered in my ear as he pulled me to the side of the pool.

I held on, unable to pull myself up with all the weight.

"What are you doing here?"

"I need to speak to Elodie."

"Are you a reporter?"

"I'm a park ranger," I said. And then a thought popped into my head. "Tell her it's Rylie Cooper, and I have what she was looking for."

"Everything okay over there?" the man from the dog side of the fence yelled.

"Yes," the big man who still had a gun pointed at me said. "I've got it under control. No need to call the police."

I didn't know if that was good for me or bad.

"Okay," the man with the dog said. "Goodnight."

The neighbor probably knew how much power the Marquez's had. I wondered how many other things the neighbor had turned a blind eye to.

"Get out of the pool," the man said.

I tried but failed. "My clothes are drenched. Are there stairs? A ladder?"

He took my hood with his free hand and pulled me like a dog on a leash. I shuffled my hands along the side of the pool until I came to a ladder.

My ankle crumpled when I took the first step. If he hadn't still been holding onto my hood, I would have gone back under.

I tried again with my other foot first, then used my arms to hoist myself up.

I folded onto the concrete and pulled myself the rest of the way.

"Graceful," I heard the guy mutter.

"I want to see you break your ankle, get humped by a horny dog, jump a fence, fall in an ice-cold pool fully-clothed, and then get out gracefully."

He let out a small laugh.

"Yeah, really funny," I said. "Are you going to shoot me, or can you put that thing away?"

He put the gun back into a holster under his jacket and helped me to my feet.

"Who did you say you were?" he asked.

"Rylie Cooper," I said through chattering teeth. "I'm a park ranger, and I have what Elodie is looking for."

"You better not be making this up. Mrs. Marquez doesn't like to be disturbed."

Mrs. Marquez? I'd have to ask her about that.

He led me inside the warm house, where I proceeded to drip all over the marble floors.

"I'll go talk to Elodie." He grabbed a pool towel out of a cabinet. "Dry yourself off. And the floor too."

I wrapped up in one of the towels and grabbed another from the closet to put under my feet.

From where I stood, I could see all the way through the house to the entry where a huge mahogany door stood between two large potted trees. To my right was the large kitchen—no takeout bags were visible, though Cedric could have eaten anywhere—and to my left was a sitting room. Photographs lined the walls. Most of them of Elodie and Jacob. Some of the people I didn't recognize.

But one caught my eye.

A picture of Selena standing in front of the mahogany door.

The top portion of the photograph had been distributed to all the news sources the night she'd gone missing—it was the one they'd flashed on the screen every chance they got. But this one showed her entire body from her long brown hair—probably a wig—all the way down to her red shoes.

Those damned shoes.

Except.

When I looked closer, something was off.

I was no shoe expert, but the red shoes she had on and the one I'd found at the reservoir and under Desmond's bed weren't the same.

The ones on her feet in the photograph were sexier with straps that crisscrossed across the top of the foot. The others were simple red pumps.

"What can I do for you?" I heard a cold voice from behind me. I couldn't tell if it was the same voice from the recording or not.

"I wanted to talk to you about Jacob," I blurted out.

"Are you having an affair with him?" She pulled a checkbook from a drawer in the kitchen. "Do you want hush money?"

"What is it with you people paying people to be quiet?" I took another look at the photograph. "I'm not having an affair with your husband—or rather —boyfriend."

When I looked back at her, her face was angry. "We're practically married."

"Is that why you call yourself Mrs. Marquez?"

"Jacob doesn't seem to mind."

I seriously doubted that. "Why *aren't* you married? Is he still hooked on Selena?" I pointed at the picture.

"He only keeps that photo up to remind himself to be better."

"Be better how?"

"Do you see the mark on her cheek?" She came to stand next to me. "He put it there."

"I know," I said.

"You do?"

"Jacob told me." I turned to her. "If you love him so much, why did you take back your statements confirming his alibis?"

"It wouldn't be right for me to lie anymore," she said, examining her beautifully manicured nails.

The guard who had brought me in looked down at his feet.

"I agree." I turned my attention from him to Elodie. "It wouldn't be right to lie."

She shifted from one foot to another. "Can we sit down? Nine months of pregnancy has made me quite tired, and my massage today will be for nothing."

We sat at a small table overlooking the back yard.

"Did you get your nails done today too?" I asked.

She smiled. "I did. I needed one last spa day before the baby came."

"What else does a spa day entail?" I asked. If she was

at the spa all day, she wouldn't have been the one who destroyed my car with Cedric.

"Massage, facial, manicure, pedicure, you know, the works."

"Sounds like a fun day. Long, but fun."

"Definitely long and much needed after finding out my husband killed his first wife."

I frowned. She wasn't a good actress. The police had to have seen right through her when she took back her alibi.

"I hear you have what I'm looking for," Elodie said.

I smiled. "I do." Now I knew she was bluffing—just saying whatever she could to get what I had. What she didn't realize was that I didn't have anything. I almost laughed.

"Is it with you?"

"I'm not that stupid," I said. "And it's a good thing I don't since I fell in your pool."

"Right, because it would have been damaged."

Her acting skills definitely sucked.

"But I don't appreciate you destroying my car to find it. You could have just asked."

"And you would have turned it over to me?" She stared at me.

"Maybe." I shrugged.

"When can you get it to me?"

"When will you stop lying to the police?"

"Why do you care so much about Jacob if you're not having an affair?"

"Why *don't* you?" I asked. "You're the one having his baby."

She ran a hand over her belly, her eyes glazing over with tears.

"You'd think that'd afford me some privileges, wouldn't you?" Her face transitioned from sadness to anger. "But no. Since he doesn't hit me, I don't get his name. I don't get the apology gifts. Trust me, I'd take a slap across the face every now and then for a pair of the custom shoes he bought her."

"That's messed up," I said. "He's trying to be a better man."

"Yeah, like when he announced to everyone that we were having a boy when I hadn't even told my family yet?"

"He made a mistake," I said.

"Like how he killed his first wife."

I narrowed my eyes. "Do you *really* think he killed her?"

She didn't respond.

"That's what I thought." I stood up. "But you realize when they find out Jacob didn't kill Selena and Desmond, you won't have an alibi either. You'll be the next suspect."

She crossed her arms across her chest. "Why would I have killed them?"

"Selena's easy. I'm sure you killed her so you could have Jacob all to yourself—apology gifts and all."

"He was going to leave her."

"Was he though?" I asked. "I bet if somehow she was still alive and came back, Jacob would drop you in a second."

"Well, she's not alive, so it doesn't matter."

"You seem confident in that fact."

"I saw the crime scene. There's no way she lived." As hard as she tried to act tough, she was getting flustered.

"They didn't find a body, so I guess you never know." I kept my voice calm.

"They found her arm. I'd say that's enough to be certain."

"I guess you better hope so." I shrugged. "Where were you the night Desmond was murdered?"

"Here," she said. "Asleep."

"Did you take a sleeping pill too?"

"Of course not." She looked down at her stomach. "I'd never do anything to hurt the baby."

"But Jacob did. So he wouldn't have known whether you were in bed or not, right?"

"Other people can attest to my whereabouts."

"Like Cedric?" I asked.

"No, not *Cedric*." She said his name with pure hatred. "I have my own security."

"These people who can confirm your alibi—are they all under your employ?" I knew it wouldn't be beneath her to pay someone to lie.

"I didn't do it. I'm pregnant. How would I have killed him?"

"It doesn't take much to fire a gun."

She stopped talking and stared at me. Her security guard stood with his gaze firmly on the floor. He'd been trained well.

I stood. "Tell the police the truth, and I'll give you what you're looking for."

"What if I don't?" she asked.

"Then I'll destroy it."

She said nothing, and I couldn't read the look on her face.

"I'll be going now."

"Maurice, take her home," Elodie said.

The man who pulled me from the pool led me to the giant door. Before I stepped outside, I paused at the spot Selena stood the last time anyone saw her.

"She deserves justice," I muttered under my breath.

"Mmm-hmm," Maurice grunted, opening the door to a shocked Luke.

"What are you doing here?" Luke asked. "Never mind. I don't want to know."

I pushed past him only to find myself facing a bunch of cameras just outside the front gates. "Damnit."

"I'll take Ms. Cooper home," Maurice said, stepping between Luke and me.

"I have questions for her," Luke said. "She can come with me."

"What questions?" I asked. "I just came to talk to Elodie."

"After trespassing in another person's yard?"

"I don't know what you're talking about," I lied.

"Why are you soaking wet?"

"That's my fault," Maurice said but didn't elaborate.

Luke ran a hand through his hair. "If this wasn't my last shift, I'd care. But I'm tired of worrying about you." He turned away. "Take care, Rylie."

A piece of my heart broke off like an iceberg crashing into the sea.

He was angry with me.

And he was leaving.

"Ready?" Maurice said.

I watched Luke walk past the cameras—a hand up, indicating he wasn't going to give them a statement.

"Why are you taking me home?" I asked.

"The last thing Mr. and Mrs. Marquez need are those vultures getting a statement from you."

"What makes you think I'd give them a statement?"

"Will you?"

I shrugged. "Maybe." I wouldn't, but I had no other way to get home. And this way, I could ask him about Elodie's alibi.

"Come on." He led me to the huge garage that could have comfortably housed all five of the Escalades Jacob leased, but only three were there.

"Where are the other cars?" I asked.

He looked at me out of the corner of his eye.

"Jacob told me he leases five of them."

"Cedric has one," he said. "The other's in the shop."

My ears perked up. "How long has it been in the shop?"

"A month." He opened the passenger door of the nearest SUV and motioned for me to get in. I was starting to rethink this. Obviously, it would have been safer going with Luke. Why hadn't I just gone with Luke?

"It's okay. I'm not going to hurt you. The cop knows I have you."

That was true. I got in.

The garage and the gates both opened automatically, and we drove out past the slew of reporters.

Luke had already gone.

"Where was she the night Desmond was shot?" I asked.

He didn't take his eyes off the road. "With me."

"Where?"

"Here. At home."

"You live at the Marquez residence?"

"I meant her home."

"Is that the only place you were?"

He sighed.

"You can tell me," I said. "I'm not the cops."

"You work with the cops."

"Not anymore, I don't," I said. "You saw back there. Luke and I aren't exactly on good terms."

He didn't respond.

"Did she kill him?" I asked.

"What do you have that she's looking for?"

"If you're honest with me, I'll be honest with you," I said. What did I have to lose?

He didn't look at me.

"I could tell you wanted to say something back at the house. You don't like lying for her, do you?"

"I didn't know she would kill him," he said, a tear in his voice. "I thought we were just going to scare him."

"We?"

"She said she wanted to get him to leave town."

I pointed for him to turn.

"Then she pulled out that gun."

"Did she kill Selena too?"

"And now I'm just as responsible as she is." He wasn't listening to me anymore. "But I can't say anything. I can't go to jail. They'll kill me in jail. The only reason I'm alive is because Mr. Marquez saved me from the gang."

"Whoa, whoa. Stop," I said, laying a hand on his arm.

He yanked his arm away. "I shouldn't have told you anything."

"You're not just as responsible. You didn't pull the trigger. You didn't even know she was going to."

"But I went. I knew she was up to something."

"She's your employer. And it sounds like you can't afford to lose this job."

He glanced over at me. "Why did I tell you?"

"Because I would tell you something in return."

"Don't bother. I don't want to know." He pulled the car over. "Just get out."

"But I'm soaking wet," I said. "And my apartment is miles away."

He turned his gaze toward me. The look in his eye was dangerous.

"Okay, I'll call an Uber." I hopped out. "But I'm also calling the police to tell them what happened."

"Don't bother. I'm turning myself in tonight."

"Turning yourself in?" I asked. "But you didn't do anything. You were just there."

Before I could even close the door, he hit the gas and tore away from the curb.

I pulled out my phone to find it dead—whether from a low battery or the dip in the pool didn't matter. I had no way to call an Uber. Or anyone.

I shoved it back in my pocket and began to hobble

down the street, every second step like a bolt of lightning shooting up my leg.

Being after midnight, there wasn't a single car on the road. All the businesses that lined the street were closed. My only option was to walk to a gas station and hope they'd let me use their phone.

But halfway down the block, a car pulled up next to me.

"Want that ride now?"

I nearly cried when I saw Luke behind the wheel.

He cranked the heat when I slid in, my arms wrapped around me.

"Th-thanks," I said through chattering teeth. "I thought you'd given up on me."

"I did too," he said. "I'm leaving in two days. I need to give up on you."

"You don't have to leave." The cold seeping into my bones was making me emotional.

"Yes. I do." He didn't look over at me.

I didn't respond. I didn't have it in me to fight him anymore.

"But while I'm helping you, I want you to know something."

"What?" I asked.

"The arm your kids found wasn't the arm Selena was using at the time of her death." Luke turned down the road toward my apartment. "She had to get a new one because she'd lost so much weight with the cancer treatment. The one we found was reported missing after a break-in at the Marquez residence several years ago."

"How long have you known this?"

"Basically, from the beginning. I think that's why Detective Bryant didn't want you helping. There was no case. Not really. Other than the shoe, maybe."

"The shoe wasn't the same as the pair Selena wore the night she disappeared," I said. "I saw a picture of her at Jacob and Elodie's house, and the shoes are definitely different."

"We suspected the shoes were planted too. Though we suspected they were just good reproductions."

"Then why was Jacob arrested for Selena's murder?"

"Like I said, there wasn't a case. We knew the evidence was probably planted."

"By Desmond," I said.

"Yes. We found the matching shoe in his closet."

"In his closet?" I asked. "Not under the bed?"

Luke turned his gaze on me for a moment, his eyes suspicious.

"I'm just surprised he'd have left them out somewhere the police could easily find them, that's all."

"Uh-huh." He didn't believe me, but he let it go. "We found the shoe in his closet the night he was killed."

If the police were there when I was there, someone else must have been in the house with me. They must have moved the shoe while the police were chasing me. The noise I'd heard hadn't been a cat.

"You okay?" Luke asked.

I didn't respond. I would bet it was Elodie or Maurice in the house that night. And if she had seen me, she probably would have shot me too.

Was she setting it up to look like Desmond killed

Selena? Why would she move the shoe? To be sure the police found it?

"Maybe I should take you to the hospital." Luke's voice was worried. "You could have hypothermia."

"I'm fine," I said. "This is all just a lot. You were going to tell me why Jacob was arrested."

"Right. Well, that was thanks to you."

"Me?"

"You and Elodie," he said. "Elodie recanted on confirming Jacob's alibi, which allowed us to bring him in."

"Didn't Cedric confirm it too?"

"From what we can tell, Cedric has gone on his monthly hiatus."

"That sounds ominous."

"Since we came into contact with Cedric, he's taken a monthly hiatus."

"And you just let him?" I couldn't tell whether Luke knew Cedric went to Florida for the non-profit. "What if he's the real killer?"

"You clarified that for us. Your recording of Jacob talking about the night of Selena's murder was enlightening."

"How?"

"Let's just say his original story was very different from what he told you." Luke pulled into my apartment complex as the sun was lifting over the horizon.

"And that was enough to arrest him for murder?"

Luke shrugged.

"What if I told you he didn't murder Desmond?"

"He still could have killed Selena."

"Maybe," I said. "But I'm leaning toward Elodie or Cedric on that one."

"Not Desmond?"

"Desmond wanted justice for his sister," I said. "Not for her to die."

Luke looked out his window so all I could see was the back of his head.

"Thanks for the ride," I said.

"The guys are throwing me an impromptu going away party tonight if you want to come." He turned to face me. His eyes were sad.

"Where?" I asked.

"At the wings joint."

"I'll be there." I pushed his shoulder and smiled. "I'd never miss a good party."

He smiled back.

I would miss that smile.

"And by the way, thanks for telling your mom I was leaving. It took everything I had in me to get her off the phone."

I laughed. "Serves you right."

A pile of mail and a tired Fizzy were on the bed I felt like I hadn't slept in for weeks. I scratched my dog behind his ears and stripped out of my wet clothes. Yoga pants and a sweatshirt never felt so good. I plugged in my phone, hoping it was only dead because of lack of battery rather than from the water.

My eyes were heavy as I thumbed through the envelopes. It was mostly bills. Cherry Anne's car payment was due, twisting a knife I didn't realize had been buried so deeply into my heart.

I threw the mail on the floor and let sleep take over.

When I woke up, it was dark, sending my brain into a state of confusion. I'd come to bed when it was just getting light outside.

I checked the time. Luke's party was in an hour. I'd slept all day.

I rubbed the sleep from my eyes and forced myself out of bed. The floor was cold and covered in mail. I reached down to pick it up when a small envelope caught my eye. I hadn't seen it the night before, and it didn't have a return address.

Inside was a photograph and a plane ticket.

The photograph was aged and blurry, but I could easily make out Cedric and Selena hand in hand, their eyes locked and smiles on their faces. It had to be an older photograph because the tattoo from Cedric's neck was missing. That, and Selena was still alive.

On the back of the photograph was a note:

Go find the truth, Rylie.

The plane ticket was for the next morning.
To Tampa, Florida.

I showered as quickly as possible, considering all the reasons someone would send me an airplane ticket. Was it from Desmond? Did he want me to go down and investigate the non-profit? And why would he have sent this to me rather than just telling me over the phone?

The flight didn't leave until nine the next morning. I had time to think about it.

I blow-dried my hair, put on a coat of eyeliner and

mascara, and found the cleanest pair of jeans from the floor vowing to get my laundry done when I got home.

My mind went to the check in my jacket pocket. I pulled it out and stared at it. One hundred thousand dollars would make quite a difference in my life, especially with my car payment looming.

But I couldn't cash it. It wasn't right.

I tore it into pieces and tossed them into my wire garbage can.

I shoved the photo and ticket I'd gotten in the mail into my back pocket and checked my phone. It was still dead. First Cherry Anne, then my phone. What was next? My apartment burning down?

On the counter was a set of keys and a note from Shayla.

Garrett ordered you a rental car. It's the blue Mazda in the parking lot. See you tonight.
-Shay

The bar was packed when I arrived. Luke was a popular guy.

"Can I sit with you?" I asked a sad-looking Nikki offering her one of the two beers I'd ordered from the bar.

She took it and nudged a bar stool my way.

"I can't believe he's leaving," she shouted over the noise.

"Me neither," I said. "I'm surprised you came."

"It wouldn't be right for me to miss it. We did date for a while."

Something in her eyes told me she hoped he would stay. "Have you seen Luke?"

"He's over by the bar, I think," she said, and when I looked, he was exactly where she pointed.

"Can I sit?" An Italian voice said behind me.

Nikki nodded, and Antonio sat next to me.

"You look flushed," Nikki said to him.

"I was chasing naked guy," Antonio said, raising his beer to his lips.

"Did you get him?" she asked.

"Nope, not that I really wanted to."

We all laughed.

"I hear you helped police nail the murderer," Antonio said.

"They got the wrong guy," I said.

Nikki and Antonio both gave me questioning looks.

"You'll see," I said. Elodie's guard had either already turned himself in or would soon. "I need to use the restroom."

I downed the rest of my beer and made my way through the crowd veering slightly toward where Luke was.

When I was about four feet from him, I noticed his smile fade. People were between us, so I couldn't see who he was talking to.

I pushed through a group of women who had obviously already had too much to drink.

Luke was chatting with Shayla, who was still in full

uniform. He nodded and began following toward the doors leading outside.

My bladder could wait. I needed to hear what they were talking about.

They walked out one set of doors through an entry hallway and then outside.

I followed but not too closely.

Once they were outside, I cracked the door just enough to hear.

"I have to arrest her," Shayla said. "I can't believe it, but I have to."

"Do you really think she did it, Shayla?" Luke asked. "This is Rylie we're talking about. Your best friend. My—"

"Why else would she have spoken to him minutes before he died but not said anything to anyone about it?"

How did they know he talked to me?

"How do you know it was his phone? They never recovered a phone from the scene."

Shayla hesitated.

"Bryant pulled her phone records, didn't he?"

"He had to. She wouldn't tell us anything," Shayla said, though her voice wasn't convinced.

My heart was beating so loudly, I was surprised they couldn't hear it.

"She got a call the night the fire department showed up at our house. The night Desmond was murdered," Shayla said. "She told me it was Garrett. But it wasn't. And the number that called her was the same number that called 9-1-1 about gunshots at Shadow Trail."

"If she killed him, why would she call 9-1-1?" Luke asked.

"*I* don't think she killed him. I know Rylie just as well as you do. But my TO and Bryant don't." She paused. "We also found something in her bedroom."

My first reaction was anger. I couldn't believe they were going through my room.

My second was panic. They'd found the check.

I had to get out of there.

I slipped back inside the crowded bar. There had to be a back exit. Through the kitchen or something.

I pushed through the groups of people laughing and drinking. If only I'd have stayed out of it. They all warned me. But I had to be a stubborn idiot.

When I found a door, it was rigged with an alarm system. In big red letters it said, Push in Case of Emergency. The door may or may not have been connected, but I couldn't just stand there and get arrested. I had to go somewhere.

I couldn't go to our apartment or Garrett's. Those were the first places they'd look. My parents' house was off the table too.

I'd figure it out once I was safely behind the wheel. Of the car Shayla knew I was driving. Damnit.

Surely, they had someone watching the car in the lot just in case I slipped by Shayla.

I'd have to walk. There was a light rail stop not too far from the bar. I could determine where I was going if I made it that far.

"Here goes nothing." I sucked in a breath and pushed the door open.

Nothing happened. No alarms. No flashing lights.

I let out the air in my lungs and slipped outside. When the door was nearly closed, the alarms blared.

Panic inside the bar was loud enough you could hear it beyond the closed door and cinderblock walls. I could just imagine all the cops reaching for their concealed weapons.

I had to get to the light rail before they found me.

I looked around to make sure there weren't any cops in view before hobbling away from the building and onto the sidewalk.

It wasn't the nicest part of town. People loitered on the streets drinking and smoking and doing who knew what else. But at that moment I didn't care, the people meandering down the sidewalk gave me somewhere to hide. If I was the only one walking down the street, I'd be easily recognized.

The train arrived just as I reached the stop.

I hopped on and prayed no one would check me for a ticket.

I pulled the hood up on my jacket and sat in one of the seats furthest back.

I had no phone. No car. Nowhere to go.

Part of me considered turning myself in. I had nothing to hide. I hadn't killed anyone.

But my actions made me look suspicious.

Very suspicious.

And if they could pull the data from my phone, they'd know I was at the scene of Desmond's murder.

I glanced up at the sign that showed the rail route. It went all the way to Denver International Airport.

The ticket to Florida was still in my pocket.

Sleeping in an airport sucked. Sleeping in an airport knowing the cops were looking for me sucked even more.

My flight didn't leave until nine in the morning, making for a long night. By the time the sun peeked up over the horizon, I was in full freak-out mode.

Every person seemed to be watching me. Even the barista at Starbucks gave me a weird stare.

I only had a little bit of time left before I'd be on an airplane and out of the state. I had to find something in Florida that would exonerate me. Maybe Cedric could confirm that Elodie killed Selena too.

Or maybe I could find proof that Cedric did. They looked awfully cozy in the photo I'd gotten.

Could he have killed her because she wouldn't leave Jacob? Guilt would explain him setting up a non-profit in her memory.

"Rylie?" Luke's voice startled me so badly I nearly

spilled my coffee down my front. I turned to run, but he caught me by the arm.

So much for me being vigilant. Now I was going to jail.

"Luke, look. I didn't kill anyone. Please don't arrest me."

Luke stood in front of me, a single bag flung over one shoulder. He wasn't there to arrest me. He was there to leave.

He dropped the bag to the ground and pulled me into a hug. "I know you didn't kill anyone. Bryant's on a witch hunt."

"I'm not a witch," I said, trying to lighten the mood even though tears were blurring my vision.

He let me go. "I'm so sorry I couldn't help more."

"I was stupid. But I'm going to get this figured out. I'll clear my name."

Luke shook his head. "You're impossible. I hope marriage settles you down a bit."

The mention of my marriage coming out of Luke's mouth made me nauseous.

"My flight's boarding," Luke said. "I have to go."

"I'll miss you."

He opened his arms, and I fell into them. The tears were flowing now.

Luke pressed his lips to the top of my head. "You know, I always thought we'd end up together. Somehow."

I nodded. "I did too."

He pulled back and looked down into my eyes. For a moment I thought he might kiss me. And for a moment I thought I might let him.

"Garrett's a lucky guy. Don't ever let him forget that."

Emotions flooded through me like a tidal wave. I sobbed as Luke turned and walked away.

I cried the entire flight. My thoughts were all over the place—sadness for losing Luke, guilt for feeling the way I did about Luke while I was engaged to Garrett, anger for being a wanted fugitive.

By the time I landed, the man next to me couldn't get up quickly enough.

I didn't care.

I stared out the window until I was the last person on the plane.

"Ma'am, are you going to get off the airplane?" a female flight attendant asked.

I stood on shaky legs.

"Whatever it is, I'm sure it'll all work out," she said as I passed her.

"Thanks," I managed.

"When I got past security, I headed in the direction of where the taxis sat anxiously awaiting their next customer.

"Rylie Cooper?" A voice to my left said.

I turned to find a woman holding a sign with my name on it. She was probably in her fifties and looked not the slightest bit intimidating.

"Who's asking?" I said.

"I have a car waiting for you," she said, directing me toward the doors. "Do you have any luggage?"

"Nope, just me."

"Very good."

She led me to a black Escalade where another woman stood holding the door open.

"Who do you work for?" I asked her before getting into the car.

"Ah, yes. I assumed you would have questions. Mr. Walden asked me to give you this." She handed me a large envelope.

"Who is Mr. Walden?"

"He's a private investigator hired by Mr. Pratt."

"As in Desmond Pratt?"

"Yes. May his soul rest in peace." She made the sign of the cross over her chest.

"Did Mr. Walden send me the plane ticket?"

She nodded. "On Mr. Pratt's direction. Mr. Pratt was convinced you'd come."

"I guess he was right," I said.

I stepped into the car, and the woman chauffeur closed the door. But she didn't make it to the driver's seat before the car lurched forward.

"Whoa, slow down," I said, looking at the driver.

"What are you doing here?" Cedric asked, his face filled with rage.

Cedric raced through Tampa traffic dodging cars, narrowly missing their bumpers.

"I asked what you're doing here," he said again.

Panic flooded me.

"I got a note and a plane ticket." Why hadn't I told anyone I was coming? Or at least gotten a replacement phone?

"From who?" He dodged between two semi-trucks making my stomach clenched.

"No return address," I said. I wasn't about to give up the PI's name.

"That little twerp needed to learn to mind his own business. If he had, he might still be alive."

"Desmond?" I asked. "But you didn't kill him, Elodie did."

Cedric glanced at me in the rearview mirror, surprise on his face. "How do you know?"

"Maurice told me," I said. "He was driving me home when he spilled."

"You really don't know how to stay out of other people's business, do you?" He looked back at the road. "I can't believe out of all the women Garrett could have chosen, you're the one he wants to marry."

"All the women? What are you talking about?" His comment took me aback. I wasn't expecting him to bring up Garrett.

"Women have always loved him. He's a handsome guy with a steady job." He turned another corner. "Don't tell me you don't see it."

"Of course, I see it. That's why I'm with him. Well, that and because I love him, of course," I added quickly. "I just didn't realize other women were banging down his door."

"He would never tell you. He's a gentleman like that."

Cedric's anger seemed to have faded.

"Is this your car?" I asked.

He laughed. "From the look on that woman's face, did it look like this was my car?"

I imagined the chauffer's shocked expression as her car drove away without her.

"You shouldn't steal other people's cars."

"Where was she going to take you?" he asked.

"How am I supposed to know? All the photograph said was go find the truth."

"Photograph?" Cedric's eyes narrowed. "What photograph?"

"The one of you and Selena," I said.

"So he did get it to you."

"Is that what you were looking for?"

He turned a corner too sharply, running over a curb. "What are you talking about?"

"When you trashed my car. Were you looking for the photograph?"

He didn't answer right away. We turned down a couple more streets and then onto a bigger highway.

"How did you know it was me?"

"My phone was still recording audio. When you freaked out about the pepper spray, I knew. You also went to Desmond's house, before he died, I presume?"

Cedric didn't respond.

"But why didn't you go to my apartment?" I asked. "You would have found the photo there."

"Break into a police officer's apartment? I may be crazy, but I'm not an idiot."

I'd have to thank Shayla when I got back. If she didn't arrest me.

"What else do you know?" Cedric asked.

I was torn. Did I tell him the information I had? If I did, he'd know what I didn't have. But maybe he could fill in some of the gaps.

"Jacob was abusive," I said. "He told me himself. He and Elodie were having an affair long before Selena died."

Cedric didn't make any actions to confirm or deny.

"The night of the gala, they fought. I don't know whether it was about his affair with Elodie or her affair with you."

Cedric didn't say anything.

"But I'm guessing it was about her and you, and that's why he hit her. And why he wouldn't let you drive her to the gala. Instead, he made you take him to see Elodie—even though she's refuting that now."

"What?" He looked slightly panicked.

"That's why they arrested Jacob for murder. She told the police she lied about confirming his alibi."

"I knew we couldn't trust her," he said. "I've hated her from the moment he hired her."

"That's the night Selena died." I hesitated. "Or went missing. Desmond seemed to think she was still alive, but from what I've heard, the scene wasn't one someone would walk away from."

Tears hung in the corners of Cedric's eyes.

"And since you and Selena were involved, you started a non-profit in her honor."

His gaze shifted to me for a long second and then back to the road again. I didn't dare bring up the idea that he might have killed Selena.

"Years went by. The police dropped the investigation after finding no evidence that led them anywhere. But Desmond wasn't okay without answers," I said. "At some point, he broke into the Marquez residence and stole Selena's extra prosthetic and possibly a pair of red shoes."

Cedric nodded, confirming at least part of my theory.

"He planted them at the reservoir where Jacob runs every day." I paused. "I'm not sure if he did it to frame Jacob or just to get the police to investigate again, but after he tipped off the press, the police had no other option but to reopen the case."

I took a breath before continuing. Outside, palm trees lined the highway along with various strip malls, car repair shops, and hole-in-the-wall restaurants.

"At this point, I'm not completely sure what happened," I said. "For some reason, Elodie killed Desmond after Jacob had taken a sleeping pill and gone to bed for the night. She and Maurice followed him to Shadow Trail Reservoir—where he planned to meet me. They rammed his car over and over before he jumped out, hopped the fence, and was shot. Elodie must have shot him through the fence."

"Any idea why she would have killed him?" Cedric asked.

"Probably like you said, he was annoying. He was probably harassing them, and Elodie is filled with hormones. I can't imagine how I'd feel if my boyfriend's ex-wife's murder surfaced just before I was about to have his baby." I paused. "I mean, I wouldn't kill anyone, obviously, but you know." I shrugged. "She does seem kind of crazy."

"Any other thoughts on the matter?" he asked. "Any idea who killed Selena?"

"You really loved her, didn't you?"

He didn't respond.

"I don't know who killed her. I'm leaning toward Elodie, but I think she and Jacob were together that night." I sucked in a breath. "I also considered you."

He nodded.

"But I'm starting to think that might not be the case."

The car was silent for a few miles. Cedric wasn't speeding anymore.

"Have you given this information to the police?" Cedric asked.

"Not all of it," I said. "Though I think they know more than I do."

"They're not the ones in Florida right now," Cedric said. "They've never come down here."

"I probably wouldn't have put any of it together if I hadn't seen you at that restaurant," I said. "When Garrett said you were going to Florida, I knew."

"How?"

"Desmond's board had four things circled—Shadow Trail Reservoir, Gala, Jacob, and Florida."

"He knew about the non-profit?"

"Looks like it," I said. "I just don't quite understand how that fits into the whole thing. I mean, I get that you'd start a battered women's shelter after what happened to someone you cared about, but how does that have anything to do with Selena's death?"

"She left a sizeable chunk of money for it in her will," Cedric said. "I think Desmond thought—or at least hoped —she'd leave him some money."

I thought about the tiny house he had lived in with junk everywhere compared to the Marquez mansion. "Is that why you think he tried to get back into her life? For money?"

"I'm sure some of it was about relationship," Cedric said. "But I'm guessing he thought if he could prove Jacob was responsible for her murder, her money would go to her next of kin rather than her murderer husband."

"Would it have?"

Cedric shook his head. "She left precise instructions that all of her money was to go to this." He motioned to a sign in front of a dilapidated strip mall that said Neleas. "And wasn't to go to Jacob or Desmond."

"From the looks of things, she didn't have much money to give."

He parked in front of the building and turned off the engine.

"Do you think this is where Desmond's people were going to bring me?"

"Why don't you open that and find out." Cedric pointed to the envelope the woman at the airport had handed me.

I hadn't wanted to open it in front of him, but my curiosity outweighed my caution. Inside the envelope were several additional photos of Cedric and Selena together—all taken by what looked like someone hiding in bushes. Probably Mr. Walden, the PI. The images were grainy and hard to make out, but there was no mistaking the couple.

I handed them to Cedric, and he thumbed through them with a smile. "He was watching us."

"Either that or he hired someone to watch you. But why?"

The next document looked like a copy of Selena's will, leaving three million dollars to Cedric to create the non-profit. It had been updated several months before she died. The date was circled in red ink.

"Does this date mean anything to you?" I asked, showing him the paperwork.

"That's the day Selena found out she had cancer." He took the papers. "How did he get these?"

"This looks like a copy of her life insurance." I moved

onto the next document. "The policy was also left to you. But this statement is dated a month ago. Why haven't you cashed it out?"

He reached for the papers, and I willingly handed them over. "I don't need the money. I'm sure Garrett told you he thinks I'm related to the Queen."

I laughed. "He did."

"I'm not, but don't tell him that. It's fun to keep him on his toes."

"But you could have used the money for the non-profit." I pointed to the building, which looked old and outdated. "Especially if this is all three million dollars will afford a person in Tampa, Florida."

"We're not in Tampa anymore," he said.

"Still," I said. "I know Florida's not that expensive."

"How about I show you?"

"That sounds like a great idea."

The inside of the building was a huge contrast from the outside. Where the outside looked like a run-down strip mall, the interior was warm and inviting.

The first room was a sitting area with oversized chairs, fluffy couches, and lots of throw pillows.

"This is where we meet the women. They can come day or night and speak with someone." He opened a door labeled *safe room*. "This room locks from the inside."

Inside were two sets of bunk beds—made up with lots of blankets and pillows—a couch, and a television. Abstract paintings brought color and warmth to a space that would hold scared women and children.

"It's impenetrable," Cedric said. "The door is bulletproof, and there are no windows. The lights are special lights that simulate the sun to help prevent depression."

"How do they find out about this place?"

"We advertise," he said. "But we don't advertise our address. We have a phone number they can call, and on-call drivers pick them up. The drivers will help them quickly pack their belongings and provide protection if needed."

He led me out of the room and back through the sitting area through two more heavy doors. "These are the living quarters," he said.

Rows of doors on either side of the corridor indicated they could comfortably house ten families.

"Do they live here permanently?"

"It's temporary," he said. "Our goal is to help them get settled in the real world, far from the reaches of their abusers. We also provide legal services to help them send their abusers to jail."

"This is fantastic," I said.

"And expensive."

"I bet Selena would be incredibly proud of you."

"I am," a woman said from behind me.

Cedric wrapped an arm around a beaming Selena.

"So you're the Rylie Cedric's been telling me about?"

I couldn't speak. I felt like I was looking at a ghost. "But you—I thought—"

"You thought I was dead." She smiled up at Cedric. "That was the goal."

"You've been alive this whole time? But how?"

"Let's sit down," she said. Her cheeks were fuller than they had been in the photo from the night of the gala, she'd probably put on ten pounds or so, and she was absolutely glowing. She was also not wearing a prosthetic. Her white button-down shirt had been neatly sewn at the shoulder.

She and Cedric led me down the hall past the doors belonging to residents into an office with the name Jane Hyland.

"Jane Hyland?" I asked.

"I couldn't exactly go by Selena Marquez, could I?"

My mind was still reeling. Desmond had been right. She was alive.

We sat in plush cream-colored chairs around a stylish wood and metal coffee table. Romantic white curtains hung to each side of to a large window that let in a bright stream of sunlight.

"Something to drink?" Selena asked.

I shook my head. "I'm okay."

"I hope Cedric didn't frighten you too badly when he abducted you at the airport." She looked over at Cedric and smiled. He squeezed her hand.

"He's just lucky I didn't have any pepper spray on me."

Selena and I laughed, Cedric's eyes widened.

"You are okay, though, right?"

"Better than my car," I said, raising an eyebrow. "What were you looking for?"

"The thing that brought you down here," she said. "The photograph Desmond sent you."

"The photograph of the two of you together?" I asked. "But that could have been taken any time."

"We couldn't risk it. When we found out he'd hired a private investigator, we knew those pictures would end up in your hands." Selena looked at Cedric. "And if Jacob knew I was alive—"

"I think he's changed," I said. "He doesn't seem like the man who used to be abusive."

Cedric nodded. "We've discussed coming clean. We're just not ready yet."

"But Jacob is being held for your murder," I said. "That's not exactly fair."

"The police know better than to hold him," Selena said.

Understanding flooded through me. "Jacob didn't pay them off, you did."

"I wouldn't call it paying them off," she said. "More like, funding my own witness protection program."

"If he was only being held for Desmond's murder, then they should be releasing him at any moment," I said.

"You don't think he killed Desmond?" Selena said.

"One of Elodie's guards told Rylie that Elodie killed him," Cedric told her.

"I just can't put together why," I said.

"She killed him because he knew I was alive." Selena's eyes filled with tears. "That has to be it."

"If he exposed you for being alive," I said, finally understanding, "Jacob might have left her for you."

"Not that I would have gone back to him." She squeezed Cedric's hand. "I don't care how much he's changed."

"What about the blood, though?" I asked. "Was that all part of the cover-up? Did the police pretend they had that evidence of your death?"

"Oh no, that was my real blood," Selena said, looking at Cedric with a wince. "Every time I went to the hospital, I had a friend of mine remove some of my blood. Cedric had it stored for future use."

"So you'd planned this for a while then?"

"We were going to do it before she got cancer," Cedric said. "But then she needed treatments, and those would have been harder to do under the radar."

"Plus, when I was sick, Jacob was nicer to me." Selena

shrugged.

"But then she was healthy again," Cedric said. "And when Jacob found out about us, he lost it."

"The night of the gala," I said.

Selena nodded. "I will never understand why he thought it was okay for him to have affairs, but not me."

"Probably because he thought he gave you everything you had," Cedric said.

"And in some ways, I guess he did," Selena said.

"But you made investments on your own," Cedric said.

"With your help." Selena looked at him with so much love in her eyes, I almost felt like I needed to look away.

"What's going on," Cedric said, pulling a vibrating phone from his pocket. "Whoa."

"What is it?" Selena asked, peeking over at his screen.

Cedric made some motions on his touch screen before he looked up with fire in his eyes. "We have to get you out of here."

He stood, gently pulling Selena to her feet by her one arm. "You come too."

Before I could figure out what was going on, we were out of the office, down the hallway, and out the back doors.

Behind the strip mall was a large grove of trees. Cedric and Selena ran through them on a small stone path that opened up to what looked like a park.

"Why are we running?" I asked, trying to keep up, my ankle still sore.

"We need to get to the garage," Selena yelled over her shoulder as I followed behind. "I'll explain everything once we're inside."

As we ran up and over a large hill, a mansion perched on the edge of a canal came into view. "Is that your house?"

"That's where some of the millions went," Cedric said with a smirk over his shoulder.

We reached the side of the house where a large attached garage held several black Escalades. Cedric walked up to a panel on the wall and typed in a bunch of numbers opening a high-tech key box.

"What about all the people at the shelter?" I asked as we hopped into the nearest SUV.

"It's on lockdown," Cedric started the car. "Anyone would be stupid to try and get in."

"Then why didn't we stay there?" I asked.

"We need to draw them away from Neleas," Cedric said. "Elodie has a tracker on my phone."

"What does Elodie have to do with this?" I asked.

"Jacob was released this morning." Cedric hit the gas and tore down the driveway that paralleled the canal.

"Do you think he found out Selena's alive? Do you think he's coming after us?" I asked from the backseat.

"Not Jacob," Cedric said. "Jacob's dead. That's why my phone's going crazy."

"Jacob's dead?" Selena and I asked at the same time. She looked like she might pass out in the passenger's seat.

Cedric reached out and took her hand. "From what I've gathered, the police know now Jacob didn't kill Desmond."

"So they let him go," I said, trying to piece the puzzle together. "And Elodie killed him, didn't she?"

"That's what it looks like." Cedric took a turn toward a

wide-open expanse of water.

"But why?" Selena asked.

"He must have found out you're alive," Cedric said. "And that means you're next."

"Why would she need to kill Selena?" I asked.

"Because Jacob never updated his will," Cedric said. "Selena still stands to inherit everything."

He put the car in park as we reached a marina. "We're going by boat. It's the safest way to get away from her thugs."

Cedric and Selena hopped out of the car, and I followed.

"Her thugs?" I looked around. Everything seemed peaceful—the sun was high in the sky, the smell of saltwater and boat exhaust filled the air, and seagulls squawked overhead.

I pulled off my hoodie down to a white tank top and tied my hair into a bun on top of my head.

"Elodie's family has deep roots in the mafia," Selena said. "I warned Jacob, but all it got me was a slap across the face. I guess he should have listened to me after all."

Cedric lead us down a long dock to a large boat with two engines hanging off the back. "Let's go."

I paused. "I think I'll just get an uber home," I said. "It's not like they're after me."

"They're after anyone who knows I'm alive," Selena said. "That includes you."

"But they don't know I know. I'm an innocent third party in all of this."

She tossed a black life jacket at me as Cedric fired up the engines. "Put it on. Let's go."

2 7

I stood for a moment, locked in a staring contest with Selena. This was all too much. Everyone was right. I wasn't a cop. I should have stayed in Colorado.

"Do the police know Jacob's dead?" I asked.

"We don't have time for questions right now," Cedric yelled over the sound of the engines. "Are you coming or not?"

Selena pulled off the ropes that held the boat to the dock, and the boat began to back out of the slip.

"If you're not coming, take the Escalade," Cedric said. "They can't track the car."

I nodded. That's what I'd do. I'd take it straight to the airport. I threw the lifejacket back into the boat.

I turned to run back to the car when a strange sound came from above. A tiny helicopter—or rather—a drone hovered above us.

"What's that?" I pointed to the sky.

"Get on the boat. Now," Cedric shouted.

I only had a split-second to react. The boat was pulling

out, and the drone definitely had me on camera. They knew I knew.

I ran back down the dock and jumped onto the boat. Cedric grabbed my arm to steady me as he slammed the throttle down, and the boat lurched.

Selena handed me the life jacket again, and I put it on.

"Get down," Cedric said. "Both of you. We don't want it to catch you on film."

"Why does Elodie want to kill you? Even if you're dead, she won't get the money. They weren't legally married."

"It'll go to Jacob's next of kin," Selena said. "He never wanted to have a baby with me. Claimed he couldn't have children." There were years of hurt behind her eyes. "I guess that was another one of his lies."

"I need to use your phone," I yelled to Cedric over the sound of the wind and the engines.

Cedric didn't even think twice before handing it over. I started to dial Luke's number then remembered with gut-wrenching clarity that I'd probably dialed his number for the last time. I cleared the number and dialed the police station instead.

The drone was still tailing us as we drove entirely too fast for the canal system. Other boaters yelled, flipped us off, and pointed at the no-wake signs while holding on for dear life as our wake rocked their boats. Homeowners stood on their private docks screaming, phones to their ears, probably calling the Coast Guard.

At least in jail, we'd be safe from Elodie's thugs, wherever they were.

"Hello? Is anyone there?" a woman's voice said on the other line.

"Sorry," I said, shoving a finger into my opposite ear. "It's extremely loud where I am. Can you please connect me to Detective Bryant? It's urgent."

"Can I tell him who's calling?"

"It's Rylie Cooper," I said.

"Luke's friend," she said, a smile in her voice. "I'll put him on."

I waited for a minute before the line connected. "Rylie? Where are you?"

"I know you were going to arrest me, but I didn't kill Desmond."

I thought I heard him laugh. "One of Elodie's security staff killed him. We know."

"No, you don't know," I said. "Elodie killed him. Maurice is taking the fall. Elodie killed Desmond, and she killed Jacob too."

"Jacob was just released an hour ago. How could you possibly know he's dead?"

I held the phone away from my mouth. "Cedric, where is Jacob?" I asked.

"She killed him at their house," Cedric yelled without taking his eyes off the water.

"Rylie? Rylie?" Bryant yelled into the phone. "Where are you?"

"I'm on a boat. In Florida," I said. "I can explain everything later. But you need to go to Jacob Marquez's house right now. You'll find his body."

"And how do you know Elodie killed him?"

As we turned around a corner, the canal opened into

what looked like the ocean. "Cedric got a message." Behind us, another boat was coming up fast. I squinted against the sun to see a man on the bow holding a huge gun aimed right at us. "And now she's trying to kill us too."

Cedric looked behind us at my outburst, turned back to the controls, and gave it more gas. I didn't know the boat could go any faster.

"If you're in Florida, you need to call the police down there. Or the Coast Guard," he added.

"I will," I said. "But you need to find Elodie."

I disconnected the call.

"Should I call the police?" I asked.

Cedric glanced back at Selena.

I looked over at her as she huddled next to me.

"I think it's time I was found," she said.

"Are you sure?" Cedric asked.

The boat behind us wasn't getting any closer, but we weren't pulling away from it either. It was only a matter of time before the man started shooting.

"Jacob's dead," she said. "And Elodie knows I'm alive."

Cedric nodded then turned his attention back to the water. "Call the Coast Guard. They're in my favorites."

I hit the button and waited for the line to connect. Waves crashed over the side of the boat. Selena and I were soaked.

"Coast Guard, what's your emergency?" a man asked.

"We're—uh—out in the ocean, I think." I looked over at Selena.

She held out a hand, and I gladly handed her the phone. "This is Selena Marquez. We are heading into the

Gulf of Mexico from Gulf Harbors toward the Anclote Key. There is a boat following us, and they are heavily armed. We have reason to suspect they intend to harm and possibly kill us."

Her voice was much calmer than my own would have been.

"We're in a 26-foot Twin-V catamaran. They're in a big black speedboat with two engines on the back. If you search my name, you'll come across a missing or deceased person file out of Colorado. I am no longer missing, but I am in danger."

She was silent, listening. Waiting.

My heart was pounding.

"Rylie, you know how to drive a boat, right?" Cedric yelled.

"Not a boat like this," I said. "I've never driven in the ocean."

"The gulf," Cedric corrected. "I need you to take the wheel. It's just like a rough day on the lake."

I managed to pull myself to my feet and made my way to the steering controls.

"Keep us between the channel markers." He motioned to the tall wooden poles on either side of us. "If you go outside, we could get hung up on the rocks."

I took the steering wheel.

"Don't let up on the speed. We're topped out and barely holding them off."

I sucked in a breath. I could do this. It was like Antonio taught me. I just needed to watch the water around me and feel the boat's movements, breathe, and stay out of my head.

Cedric lifted one of the seats to a storage container underneath and pulled out a large black case.

"What is that?" I yelled.

"Keep your eyes on the water," Cedric said. "This is just a little protection. Don't worry. I won't fire unless they fire first."

"The Coast Guard is on their way," Selena said. "About five minutes out."

"I don't think we have five minutes," Cedric said.

"We have to," Selena said just as the man on the other boat opened fire.

"Holy shit," I screamed. "He's going to hit us."

Bullets hit the water to each side, but none had hit the boat . . . yet.

"Your life vest is bulletproof," Cedric said. "Just keep your head down."

Oh sure. That would be easy. If only I didn't have to watch where I was going.

"Maybe you should drive," I said as another round of bullets came our way.

"Just keep going. We're almost out of the channel. Once we're out, I want you to take a hard left."

Hard left. Only a few more markers to go, and we'd be out.

Out of the corner of my eye, I saw Cedric hoist what looked like a rocket-launcher to his shoulder.

"You're going to blow them up?" I yelled.

"Have a better idea?" Cedric paused.

"Uh—"

"Didn't think so."

"But what if the shrapnel hits us?"

"That's why you'll take a hard left." He glanced over his shoulder in the direction we were heading. "Now."

I cranked the wheel hard, my boat going around the last channel marker like a barrel horse around the final barrel.

I laughed at the thought of the *horse*power needed to propel a boat this fast.

*Horse*power.

Ha!

I was losing it.

Laughing about horsepower.

"Get down!" Cedric shouted.

I held the wheel steady and dropped to my knees.

An explosion sounded behind us.

"Did you get 'em?" Selena asked.

Cedric peeked up. "Got 'em."

"Won't you be in trouble for blowing up another boat?" I asked, standing back up and quickly checking the surroundings to make sure there weren't any other boats around.

"It was self-defense," Cedric said. "We have it all on film." He pointed to a camera mounted on the canopy above my head.

I shrugged.

Cedric returned the rocket-launcher to the case, but kept the case open, then took the wheel back. "You did good."

"Thanks," I said.

"Looks like the Coast Guard finally decided to show up," Selena said, pointing to an approaching boat.

Selena and Cedric explained the entire situation to the Coast Guard, and after what had to be at least an hour, they led us back to shore, a different way than we'd come.

Cedric drove the boat with Selena next to him as I sat in the back, promising myself over and over I wouldn't get in the middle of another police investigation ever again. This was too crazy. Garrett deserved a wife whose life didn't stress him out. And I deserved—well—a life.

I was tired of getting in the middle of everything, putting my life at risk. If I was good at it, that would be one thing. But I wasn't. I didn't even know Selena was alive. I was looking for a murderer who didn't exist.

I needed to go back to being a park ranger. Heck, even managing the juvenile spring break program didn't sound too bad.

"I called you a car, and you'll have airline tickets waiting for you at the airport," Selena said when we got to shore. "Thank you for caring enough about me to go through all this trouble." She wrapped me in a hug.

"You're welcome," I said. "Desmond did too. He believed the entire time you were still alive."

She gave me a sad smile. "I guess we'll never know his true intentions."

I wanted to argue, but she knew him better than I had.

"When you get back to Colorado, call the detectives. Make sure they have Elodie in custody and that she's called off her people before you go home."

"Do you think they'll still be after me?" I asked.

"Until she calls them off, they most definitely will be."

Tears sprung to my eyes. Exhaustion was taking over my emotions.

She pulled me into another hug. "Don't worry. It'll all be okay." She held me at arm's length and smiled. "And when we get back to Colorado, we'll have to go on a double date. I can't wait to meet Cedric's best friend from college."

I smiled.

"Don't let that one go," she said. "If he's anything like Cedric says, he's one of the good ones."

"I won't." I held up my ring. "He's stuck with me."

We both laughed as the car pulled up, and the driver got out to open my door.

"Take her to the airport," Selena said.

"Yes, Miss Hyland."

"Actually, it's Mrs. Marquez," she said.

He smiled and closed the door once I was settled inside.

Selena turned back to Cedric, who was speaking with the Coast Guard.

Within seconds, I was fast asleep.

29

When I got past the security checkpoint at the Denver International Airport, I searched for a payphone to call the police station. I'd have to call collect, but it would have to do.

"Miss Cooper?" a voice said behind me.

I whipped around almost too quickly, my fists up ready for a fight.

"Whoa, stop," the scrawny man said. "I'm just here to give you this. From Miss Hyland."

I took the large envelope from his hands. "Thank you. And sorry, I'm a little jumpy."

"No problem." He turned and walked away as fast as his tiny legs could carry him.

Inside the envelope were a cell phone, a set of keys, and several hundred dollars in cash.

I closed the envelope quickly and glanced around as if I'd just robbed a bank. A few deep breaths later, I pulled out the phone and turned it on. It was the newest model with all the bells and whistles.

Programed into the contacts were a few names—Selena, Cedric, and Detective Bryant.

I tapped on the one for Detective Bryant and waited for him to answer.

"Bryant," he said in a gruff voice.

"Hi, yeah, it's Rylie," I said.

"Made it back to Denver?"

"At the airport now," I said. "I was supposed to call you and tell you that Elodie needs to call her people off."

"Selena already called," he said. "It's taken care of."

"Wait," I said. "You don't sound surprised that Selena is alive."

He didn't respond.

"You knew all along, didn't you?" I felt even more like an idiot now. "That's why you wanted me to stay out of it. You were protecting her."

"I have to go," he said. "Next time, trust me."

He disconnected the line. A weight lifted from my shoulders.

I was done with police work. Done with interfering. I would take my money and whatever car Selena had rented for me and go straight home.

A note was inside the envelope beneath all the cash.

Rylie,

Thank you for all of your help. You have a talent for investigation. Don't let anyone tell you differently. I'm sorry about your car. I've bought you a replacement—or rather— an upgrade. I've also provided supplemental pay for the time you had to take off work, plus a bit more. If you ever

need anything, please let me know. And call me for that double date.
Thank you again,
SM

I pulled the keys out and looked them over more carefully. They looked like a typical key fob, but when I turned them over, a familiar horse sent excitement racing through my veins.

I ran through the airport to the parking garage and clicked the panic button to determine which one was mine. A bright red, brand new Mustang convertible sat right up front. And every time I clicked the button, it sounded an alarm.

I clicked the unlock button, and the car unlocked. I opened the door and slid into the supple black leather seats with red stitching. The glorious new-car smell filled my nose, making me salivate almost as if it was the smell of freshly-baked cookies.

I could have cried. This car had to have cost thousands more than Cherry Anne and the title—sitting on the passenger seat—had my name on it with a sticky note that said: Paid in Full.

Now, I did cry.

All the way back to my apartment.

30

"I've been worried sick," Shayla said when I walked into the apartment, wrapping me up in her arms. "Jacob's dead, and Elodie's in the hospital."

"Why is she in the hospital?" I asked. "She's the one who killed Desmond and Jacob."

"She's in labor," Shayla said. "But then she'll go to prison. For a long time."

"She tried to kill me too," I said. "While I was in Florida."

"I heard," Shayla said, hugging me again. "And I heard you found out about Selena."

"Did you know?" I sat on the couch.

Shayla looked at the ground. "I couldn't tell you."

"I know," I said. "I'm sorry I interfered. My investigation days are done."

"I still think you'd make an incredible officer. And eventually, investigator."

I shook my head. "Too dangerous."

A knock at our front door propelled me to my feet.

When I opened it, Garrett embraced me so tightly, I could hardly breathe. Tears of relief and happiness came to my eyes.

"I couldn't get hold of you," Garrett said, his voice laced with emotion. "I thought something had happened to you."

Guilt coursed through me. Something almost *had* happened to me. He would have been crushed.

"I'm so sorry. I'm done investigating. I'm perfectly happy being a normal park ranger."

"Promise?"

I pulled back and looked up into his eyes. "I promise."

He bent down and kissed me gently at first and then with growing passion. Eventually, Shayla excused herself from the room, leaving Garrett and I to get reacquainted.

I woke up the next morning on the couch, wrapped in Garrett's arms. His face had a long pillow line across it, and his hair pointed in all different directions, but none of that changed how handsome he was and how lucky I felt.

My phone buzzed on the table. It was an incoming call.

I snatched it up and carefully covered Garrett with the blanket before taking the call back to my bedroom.

"Hello?" I asked.

"Is this Rylie?" the voice was familiar, but I couldn't place it.

"Yes."

"This is Ursula."

Ursula as in the Parks and Recreation Director? As in my boss? My big boss?

"Hi Ursula."

"I trust you will be back at work today?"

I almost jumped for joy to hear I'd still have my job.

"I'll have to see if the police have released my work equipment yet."

"They have. It's in my office. Please put on your uniform and meet me here as soon as you are able."

I checked the time. "I'll be there by nine o'clock."

"Perfect."

She disconnected before I had a chance to say goodbye.

I took the quickest shower known to man, tied my hair back in a braid, and put on one of my clean uniforms, minus the bulletproof vest that had been in my trunk along with my badge and duty bag.

"I have to go to work," I told Garrett before I left. "I love you."

"I love you too," he murmured. "And Rylie?"

"Yeah," I said.

"Thanks for being my fiancée."

"It's my pleasure." I smiled, but his eyes were still closed. "And tonight, let's talk about wedding plans."

"Sounds good," he said.

"Come in, close the door behind you," Ursula said when I walked in. Her long black hair was pulled up in a chic bun —one I'd never be able to accomplish on my own.

I sat in the chair across from her. Her desk was the tidiest desk I'd ever seen. All of her files were neatly stacked and alphabetized, her workspace smelled like it had just been disinfected, and there wasn't a lick of dust on her computer screen.

"Your things are in the box." She motioned to the box next to the door.

"Thank you," I said, not sure whether I should take that as a hint to stand and leave or to stay seated.

"I would like to speak with you about your behavior."

Ah, so I wasn't leaving.

"As you know, Detective Bryant informed me of your interference with law enforcement on multiple occasions."

I nodded. It was no use trying to defend myself. What he'd told her was true.

"Do you plan on continuing down this road?"

"What road?" I asked.

"The road that leads you to unemployment."

"No." I shook my head. "I don't."

"I want to make myself perfectly clear, so listen closely," she said, her voice grating. "You are not to interfere with police investigations in this city ever again. If you do, you will be terminated immediately, no matter how many cop or ranger friends you have."

"Yes, ma'am." I had no intention of sticking my nose into police business again.

"In addition to this warning, you will finish the spring break community service program every weekend until those kids get their hours. You will also be assigned to one of our newest seasonal rangers, my niece, Victoria. She starts at the beginning of June, but I'd like you to meet her today."

She motioned with her hand for someone to come in.

I turned to find a woman I'd only seen once before. I'd never learned her name.

"Rylie, this is Victoria."

Victoria's face showed no recognition of who I was. My temper flared. How dare she not remember me?

"It's a pleasure to meet you, Rylie." Her handshake felt like I was squeezing a dead fish—slimy and cold.

"The pleasure is all mine." In addition to dealing with those punky tweenagers, I'd have to spend my entire summer with her.

Giraffe girl.

THE END

If you liked this book, I'd love it if you'd write a review on Amazon or Goodreads and share it with your friends.

If you want to read short stories about giraffe girl and Rylie and Garrett's engagement, go to www. stellabixby.com.

ACKNOWLEDGMENTS

As always, I am so blessed to have a great deal of support when I write.

God, thank You for making me the person—the writer—I am.

Nolan, thank you for all your support through this crazy writing journey. You are the best husband a woman could have.

Faith, you're awesome. Don't ever forget that.

Lily, I can't wait until you read these books. I love getting your take on my books.

Grant, thank you for finally taking naps in your crib. It really helped me get things done.

Christian, thank you for sleeping more than two hours at a time every night so I could get my brain back.

Mom, thank you for always telling me the truth even when I don't want to hear it. Your input is invaluable.

Lurea, thank you for being one of my biggest fans and for your feedback. Especially, about the Florida details!

To my beta readers, you're the best. I seriously could not do this without you. You enhance my books beyond what I could imagine.

And a HUGE thank you to all of my readers. Your words of encouragement keep me going when I contemplate closing my laptop and hanging up my typing fingers. If not for you, there would be no books.

ABOUT THE AUTHOR

Stella Bixby is a native Coloradan who loves to snow-board, pluck at the guitar, and play board games with her family. She was once a volunteer firefighter and a park ranger, but now spends most of her time making up stories and trying to figure out what to cook for dinner.

Connect with Stella on Facebook, Twitter, and Instagram @StellaBixby.

Stella loves to hear from her readers!
www.stellabixby.com

www.ingramcontent.com/pod-product-compliance
Lightning Source LLC
Chambersburg PA
CBHW021656110726
47902CB00007B/1952